I

"I love the wa
There is somet

I'm someplace I m not supposed to be, seeing things
I'm not supposed to see and that is so delicious."
REBECCA FORESTER, USA Today Bestselling Author

This book "is creative and captivating. It features
bold characters, witty dialogue, exotic locations,
and non-stop action. The pacing is spot-on, a solid
combination of intrigue, suspense, and eroticism. A
first-rate thriller, this book is damnably hard to put
down. It's a tremendous read."
FOREWORD REVIEWS

"A terrifying, gripping cross between James Patterson
and John Grisham. Jagger has created a truly killer
thriller."
J.A. KONRATH, USA Today and Amazon Bestselling
Author

"As engaging as the debut, this exciting blend of
police procedural and legal thriller recalls the early
works of Scott Turow and Lisa Scottoline."
LIBRARY JOURNAL

"The well-crafted storyline makes this a worthwhile
read. Stuffed with gratuitous sex and over-the-top

violence, this novel has a riveting plot."
KIRKUS REVIEWS

"Verdict: The pacing is relentless in this debut, a hard-boiled novel with a shocking ending. The supershort chapters will please those who enjoy a James Patterson–style page-turner"
LIBRARY JOURNAL

A "clever and engrossing mystery tale involving gorgeous women, lustful men and scintillating suspense."
FOREWORD MAGAZINE

"Part of what makes this thriller thrilling is that you sense there to be connections among all the various subplots; the anticipation of their coming together keeps the pages turning."
BOOKLIST

"This is one of the best thrillers I've read yet."
NEW MYSTERY READER MAGAZINE

"A superb thriller and an exceptional read."
MIDWEST BOOK REVIEW

"Verdict: This fast-paced book offers fans of commercial thrillers a twisty, action-packed thrill ride."

PRIME
SUSPECT

R.J. JAGGER

Thriller Publishing Group, Inc.

PRIME SUSPECT

Thriller Publishing Group, Inc.

Copyright©RJJagger

Library of Congress Control Number: Available

ISBN 978-1-937888-59-6

Cover illustration by Robert A. Maguire
Used with permission.

For Eileen

DAY

ONE

August 3
Saturday

1

August 3
Saturday Night

The Bokoray on this Saturday night, like every Saturday night, was filled with sex and smoke and perfume and gyrating bodies and drunken minds and laughter and secrets and deep dark lust bubbling to the evil surface. On the stage behind the drums, with a beat in his sticks and a rhythm in his body, Bryson Wilde had the best view in the whole crazy place.

At six-two with a fit body, a Fedora dipped over his left eye, an easy smile and a face that turned heads—not to mention being a member of the band—he was well equipped to take advantage of every little thing the place had to offer.

Tequila was in his gut.

A smoke dangled from his lips.

Ashes dropped onto the snare and then sprang

wildly off when the stick came down.

His hair was blond, longer than most and combed straight back. Green eyes played well against a Colorado tan.

Directly in front of him at the microphone, Destiny Smith was busy seducing the crowd with her lamenting voice, her curvy squeeze-me body and her only-for-you eyes.

Wilde appreciated her as part of the band but otherwise didn't concentrate on her, not tonight.

He'd been there before.

She was nice; Wilde had no complaints but tonight his eyes were on the crowd. Somewhere out there was a little beauty he'd never met, an island he'd never been to, a sunrise he'd never seen.

The dance floor was packed.

The bar areas were packed.

The tables were packed.

The night was on.

A woman leaning against the wall caught his eye.

She was by herself.

She was sipping a drink.

She was throwing an occasional glance his way.

She was different. Her skin was tanner and her cheekbones were higher. Her hair was straight instead of curled, raven-black, and long—very long—halfway down her back. She wore a sultry white dress and matching heels. The next time she looked at him, he looked right back.

She didn't turn away.

Wilde tossed her a smile and then concentrated on the song; a good thing, too, because they were in the final eight bars and bringing it to a stop.

As soon as the break came, he went over.

She was waiting for him.

"Normally I'm a nice guy," he said. "Tonight I'm a bit of a jerk, so you'll have to excuse me in advance." He pulled a pack of cigarettes from his pocket, tapped two out and offered one to her. She took it and he lit her up. "I've never seen you around town. You got a name?"

"Sudden."

"Sudden?"

"Sudden Dance," she said. "I'm part Navajo. Is that a problem?"

He shook his head.

"Not for me."

"Good because it is for some."

"Their loss."

The woman had liquor in her gut and it showed when she talked.

"Tonight you're feeding the wolf," she said. "I don't mind. I do it too; too much for my own good, if the truth be known."

Wilde wrinkled his brow.

"I'm not following—"

She took his hand and examined it, then looked into his eyes. "In each of us there's a wolf and an eagle," she said. "They're constantly at battle with each other. The wolf tries to drag you down. The eagle tries to make you soar. In the end only one of them can survive. Do you know which one wins?"

He shook his head.

"The one you feed," she said.

Wilde smiled.

"I like that," he said. "The drums, they're not my full-time thing. I only do it on a fill-in basis. Nine to five I'm a private investigator. Or to put it a different way, nine to five the eagle is winning. I have a lot of eagle in me, is what I'm saying."

She wrinkled her brow and studied him in a new light.

"A private investigator?"

"Yes."

"Are you any good?"

He took a deep drag.

"Why?"

She diverted her eyes.

Wilde put a hand on hers and said, "Are you in some kind of trouble?"

She shrugged.

"I don't want to talk about it. I just want to get drunk."

Wilde nodded.

"Sounds reasonable."

He was addicted.

The woman was nice.

She was better than nice.

At the end of the evening after the final song, the last sips of alcohol slid down drunken mouths and the bodies began to stagger out. In another five minutes the house lights would come on. "I have to help the band break down," Wilde said. "It's going to take fifteen or twenty minutes. Will you wait for me?"

"Do you have a car?"

"Yes."

"Can I sit in it? I need to close my eyes so much—"

"Sure."

He gave her the key.

"It's a small green MG with a tan top parked back in the alley. It's English so the steering wheel's on the wrong side. Her name's Blondie."

She gave him a long, deep kiss and rubbed her stomach on his.

"Don't be long."

"I won't."

When he came out fifteen minutes later, the car wasn't there; neither was Sudden Dance. Both were extremely, absolutely gone.

He paced in front of the club, drawing deep on smokes and churning the possibilities.

It was possible that the whole night was nothing more than an elaborate charade to get his keys and steal his car. While theoretically possible, the prospect didn't resonate down in his gut. It didn't fit. The more likely scenario was that she decided to head out for cigarettes or something like that and then got disoriented. Or maybe she got in a wreck and then was so scared at what she'd done that she took off. Either that or the trouble she referred to so cryptically earlier in the evening had shown up to get her.

In thirty minutes she still hadn't returned.

No one was around.

The band was gone.

Everyone from inside the club was gone.

It was two in the morning.

The city was dead.

Wilde's brain was dead.

His body was lead.

Solitary headlights came up the street.

Wilde walked to the curb and stuck his thumb out.

The headlights slowed and then pulled to a stop.

DAY

THREE

August 5
Monday

2

August 5
Monday Morning

Monday morning Wilde took the bus to work and didn't like a second of it. There he paced in front of the windows with coffee in one hand and a smoke in the other, no longer giving a crap about the car.

Sudden Dance, on the other hand, was a different story.

When he closed his eyes he could smell her neck.

He could feel the smoothness of her skin on his fingertips.

He could feel the anticipation of what was on the verge of happening before it got derailed.

On his desk were several pictures of the woman.

They didn't come easy.

They came from Bob, The Big Kahuna in Denver who usually developed film for camera clubs, which were hordes of sleazy men who collectively hired a hooker or similar spirit and took naked pictures of her. Saturday night Bob was on assignment at the Bokoray taking promo photos of the band and the establishment. Wilde spent most of yesterday tracking him down and then hanging out in the man's tight little darkroom as he developed the prints. There were two rolls total. Sudden Dance showed up in five shots. If trouble had been following her it might have entered the club, so Wilde took a print of every shot, at 10-cents each.

If trouble was there it wasn't obvious.

He tossed the butt out the window and lit another one.

His office was in the 1500 block of Larimer Street, on the second floor above the Ginn Mill and two doors down from the Gold Nugget Tap Room. Directly outside his building was a water fountain sculpture with cherubs, a throwback to the area's better days.

The water didn't run anymore.

Now the bowl collected cigarette wrappers and RC bottles.

Once the retail heart of Denver, now Larimer Street and its backdoor cousin, Market Street, were an unhealthy mixture of liquor stores, bars, gambling houses, brothels and flophouses, occasionally punctuated with the sound of gunfire. If this section of Denver were a smoke it wouldn't be a Camel or a Marlboro, it would be a cigar—not the worst cigar

in the world, not the one that creeps into everything
it touches and dies an immediate stinky death, but a
cigar nevertheless.

Wilde didn't care.

He could afford better but liked it there and made
no apologies.

His watch said 8:15.

Alabama would be here in 15 minutes.

Suddenly his phone rang. The voice was one he recognized but hadn't heard in some time. It belonged
to a bomber buddy named Crazy Randy, who rode
the navigation chair on missions where Wilde worked
the guns.

"Do you still own that stupid green car with the
steering wheel on the wrong side?"

"Yes."

"Then how drunk are you getting yourself these
days?"

The question related to the fact that the man
spotted Blondie on the side of the road twenty miles
south of the city. That wasn't the issue. The car had
a flat tire. That wasn't the issue either. The issue was
that the doors were unlocked and the key was in the
ignition.

Two minutes later Wilde was in a cab heading
south.

Blondie was smack in the middle of nowhere, on a

two lane road flanked by telephone wires, awash in an endless expanse of rolling terrain that was choked with high prairie grasses, yucca, rabbit brush, moss rock and scraggly pinions. Ten miles to the west the ground rose into foothills, and beyond that the foothills escalated into mountains. To the east the geography rose and fell like ocean swells all the way to Kansas.

Wilde made sure the spare tire had air in it, and that all the parts for the jack were there and functional, before cutting the cab driver loose.

The air was silent.

High above a hawk circled.

Wilde checked the interior.

At first everything seemed normal. A closer look at the passenger seat showed there had been blood there, lots of blood, since wiped off with a cloth or something but not to the point of perfection. Dried blood was also on the side of the seat, not wiped off—missed. The black floor mats were the most telling of all, filled with pools of liquid now dried to a rusty-brown color.

Wilde's heart pounded.

He called out, "Sudden Dance!"

No one answered.

He headed into the terrain, hoping beyond hope to not find a body. Thirty steps off the road he found the white dress Sudden Dance had been wearing.

It was soaked with blood, now dried but horrific in the sheer volume of it all. Three cuts showed in the stomach area and two more near the heart, the kind you'd expect from a knife.

He swallowed.

"Sudden Dance!"

Something was on the ground next to the dress, something shiny. It was an earring. Wilde recognized it as the one Sudden Dance had been wearing.

"Sudden Dance!"

No one answered.

The body wasn't in sight.

He walked deeper into the brush, intent on finding it. It didn't show up, not in five minutes, not in ten, not in fifteen. He searched the other side of the road. It wasn't there either.

It wasn't anywhere.

He double-checked, searched a wider area and then triple-checked.

The body wasn't there.

3

August 5
Monday Afternoon

Back in Denver, Wilde made a report with homicide detective Johnnie Fingers, who listened carefully to everything, tapped a pencil and took no notes. At the end he said, "She was an Indian?"

"Part Indian," Wilde said. "I don't know how much." He slid one of Bob's pictures across the desk, tapped on the woman's face and said, "That's her right there."

Fingers studied it.

"She looks drunk."

"Yeah, she was drinking."

"Did you buy them?"

"The drinks?"

Fingers nodded.

Wilde said, "Some of them."

Fingers leaned forward. "So what did you think was going to happen, sending a drunk Indian girl into an alley in the middle of the night?"

Wilde stood up.

"See you around."

"Right," Fingers said. "See me around. Come back if you ever find a body. Until then we don't have a homicide."

Wilde paused at the door.

"He dumped it," he said.

Fingers showed his impatience.

"You said you looked around."

"I did," Wilde said. "Put yourself in his shoes. You got a dead woman in the car and then the car gets a flat. It's the middle of the night. It's pitch black out. So what do you do? You drag the body out into the brush in case some good Samaritan comes along to see if he can help. You don't want him spotting a body and calling the cops."

"You said you checked."

"Think about it," Wilde said. "You come back later and get the body. Then you dump it somewhere else, somewhere it will never be found. With no body there's no homicide. With no homicide there are no detectives chasing your ass."

Fingers narrowed his eyes.

He leaned forward.

"You sure got this all figured out," he said. "Here's how it looks from my angle. You're with a woman in a club, buying her drinks and getting all excited about bringing her home and spreading her legs. Is that much true?"

"That's a crude way to put it."

"Pa-tay-toe, pa-tah-toe," Fingers said. "Then the woman's blood ends up all over inside your car."

"Right."

"Obviously something happened."

"Yeah, someone murdered her."

"Assume that's true," Fingers said. "So far, I don't see anyone in this picture except you and her."

Wilde shook his head at the absurdity of the accusation.

"If I did it, why would I be here talking to you?"

Fingers hardened his face.

"It's called a pre-emptive strike," he said. "It happens all the time." A beat then, "Maybe she changed her mind out there in the alley about going home with you. Maybe you two had an argument. Maybe it escalated more than you thought it would. I want to get some pictures of your car. I want the dress and the earring, too."

"Sure."

Back at the office Alabama was sitting in Wilde's chair with her feet propped up, eyeballing a magazine. Wilde tossed his hat at the rack and missed by three feet. Alabama picked it up, walked over to where Wilde was and tossed a ringer.

"Tilt it to the right," she said. "We've been over this."

He set a book of matches on fire, lit a smoke and then tossed the flames in an ashtray.

Then he told Alabama everything that happened.

"Once I said the word *Indian* it was all over. I may as well have been talking about a mosquito from that point on. Fingers could have cared less about the whole thing until he started to come up with some stupid theory that I was the killer. Then he brightened up."

Alabama sat on the desk and dangled her feet.

"I don't get your obsession with this woman," she said. "It's pretty obvious she did something to bring all this on. It all came down the night you met her. It was just an hour of bad timing on your part. Move on, that's my advice. If you're right and she's dead, you can't bring her back anyway." She tapped a file next to her thigh. "You have paying cases right here. You also have a gorgeous little assistant who needs to be paid and pampered."

He took a deep drag, blew smoke and gave her one of the photos from the club.

"That's her," he said. "She's from out of town, meaning she was either staying at a hotel or with a friend, and since she was alone, my guess is the former. Find out which one. Get her last name. Find out where she was from. Get everything you can on her."

"Does this mean you're not taking my advice?"

He blew her a kiss.

"I'll take your advice when your advice starts to be that I should drink more."

DAY

FOUR

August 5
Tuesday

4

August 6
Tuesday Morning

Tuesday morning Wilde headed south out of the city, to where Blondie had been broken down yesterday, and killed the engine, on a mission that might be brilliant or dumber than dirt. Time would tell.

He got out.

The hawk was gone.

Small butterflies were everywhere.

A light breeze rustled the grasses.

As long as he was there he checked the area one more time and found everything as before.

Then he put himself in the position of the killer. He imagined pulling behind Blondie in a new car, something with a good-sized trunk. He looked around and saw no one. The body was where the dress was, thirty steps from the road. He made his way over to and smiled when he found it was still there. No one had spotted it. He picked it up, stench and all, and carried it towards the road, keeping a constant vigil in both directions to be sure no one was coming.

He got it in the trunk and closed the lid tight.

A car broke over the horizon line.

He decided to forget about the dress.

Then he headed south away from the city. What he needed was a good place to dump the little bitch, some place she'd never be found, not in a hundred years.

He'd know it when he saw it.

He kept driving.

Sunshine filled the sky.

Everything was fine.

Wilde got in Blondie and followed the trail—the *possible* trail—south. A hundred yards went by, then another and another. No roads crossed, no train tracks appeared, nothing good raised its ugly face. The topography rolled on, more and more and more of the same, none of it shouting out that right there would be the perfect place to bury a body. Then a mile down the road an abandoned road intersected from the right, almost invisible. The weeds were overgrown and undisturbed. No one had driven down it for a long, long time.

Still, someone might have walked down it.

The ruts were too deep for Blondie.

The road crested over a rise two or three hundred yards in the distance and then disappeared as it dropped into the other side.

Wilde killed the engine, lit a smoke and got out. The sunshine went straight to his brain. He patted Blondie's hood and said, "Start when I come back."

For a second he thought about turning the engine over, just to be sure it would start. The problem was, that might be the last start Blondie had left. It would be just his luck to use it up for no good reason.

He locked the doors and shoved the key in his pocket.

Then he walked west with the Fedora dipped over his left eye.

Seed barbs snagged into his socks and sawed against his skin, as irritating as mosquitoes. Every twenty steps he had to stop and pull the worst offenders out. Over the crest, another two hundred yards in the distance, a small group of dilapidated structures huddled together.

He picked up the pace.

The biggest structure, once a small house or cabin, was now nothing more than an unhealthy version of its former self. The door was gone, the windows were gone, the boards were loose and dry-rotted, and the interior had been invaded by the weather and by animals for many years, if not decades.

The other two structures, sheds, were actually in

better shape.

None of them had a body on the floor.

Out back Wilde found a narrow well, three or four feet in diameter. An odor, possibly of death, wove up from out of the darkness.

"Sudden Dance.!"

No one answered.

He dropped a rock in and got no splash, then did it again and got the same. The well was dry. It was thirty or forty feet deep, judging on how long it took the rock to land. The odor could be Sudden Dance. It could equally be an animal or nothing more than stale ground.

Behind one of the sheds, in the dirt and weeds, was a coil of old rope. Wilde freed it, stretched it out and found it to be long, a hundred feet. It was in bad condition, frail and worn.

Still, it might have enough left to hold him.

He tied one end around a rabbit brush and tugged. The anchor was good. The rope had strength. He straightened it out and tugged at it from the middle and then the end. If there were any weak links, he didn't detect them.

He lowered the rope into the well.

This wasn't smart.

If the rope broke and he got trapped, no one knew he was there. The saner thing was to come back later with proper rope, a flashlight and Alabama. That would take a lot of driving and time, though.

He tugged at the rope one final time, detected no fatal weaknesses and then positioned himself at the edge of the well.

Then he set the Fedora on the lip and began the descent.

Halfway down the rope broke.

His body went into a freefall.

Then the impact came, hard, so incredibly hard, with the force of a King Kong slap.

The air flew out of his lungs.

His brain lost focus.

Everything turned black.

5

August 6
Tuesday Morning

When Wilde regained consciousness, he found himself on top of a cold lifeless body. His first thought was that it was Sudden Dance. His second thought was that he'd rot a slow, agonizing death if he didn't get the hell out of there.

The light from above didn't filter down this far.

The body had no discernable shape.

He felt the sides of the well and found jagged rocks, the kind you get from blasting. The surface was forty feet above. The light filtered down halfway. The rope broke about fifteen feet down.

The narrowness of the shaft worked to his advantage. He was able to wedge his body against the opposite sides and muscle up one painful inch at a time until he got a hand on the rope.

Then he was out, on his back, too exhausted to stand.

The sun never felt so good.

A magpie flew overhead and eclipsed the sun as it went past.

The shadow crossed Wilde's face

It felt like cold water.

He got up.

His clothes were destroyed but didn't show any signs of dead goo. All the blood was his.

The next two hours were a flurry of motion. He found a small crossroads farming town with a general store ten miles farther south. There he gassed up Blondie, purchased two lengths of ¾" rope and the best flashlight in the store.

Then he headed back to the well and descended.

The body belonged to a woman, but not Sudden Dance.

She was naked, in her mid to late-twenties.

The cause of death wasn't apparent. No visible signs of shooting, stabbing or fighting showed.

She hadn't been dead long, two or three or four days at best.

Wilde closed her eyelids, kissed her forehead and got the hell out of there.

Back in Denver he swung by his house for a quick shower and change; then, at the office, he intentionally titled the Fedora to the right and shot for the rack.

It sailed out the window.

He ran over to see it disappearing down the street in the bed of a pickup truck. He didn't care. He wasn't stuck in the bottom of a shaft and that's all that mattered.

"Not that far to the right," Alabama said.

Wilde lit a smoke.

The air was hot.

The fan blew but seemingly in mockery of its own inability to do anything.

He told Alabama about the dead women in the well. She listed with more and more disbelief showing in her face and at the end said, "Are you sure she wasn't Sudden Dance?"

"Positive. Plus she had no blood."

"What's strange about the whole thing isn't just that she got herself dead right around the same time as Sudden Dance, but that you found her body."

"Yeah, I know."

"Are you going to make a report, to Fingers?"

Wilde nodded.

"Maybe he'll take more interest is this one, being that she's not an Indian."

"Do you think they're connected? The two killings—"

Wilde blew smoke.

"They're pretty close both in time and in place. My gut says, yes."

Alabama's face brightened. "Oh, I almost forgot," she said. "Your little friend who dances suddenly was staying at the Kenmark, Room 207. She checked in under the name S D Smith and paid upfront until Wednesday."

Wilde blew smoke and wrinkled his forehead.

"Smith my ass," he said. "Is all her stuff still in her room?"

"As far as I know."

"We need to get in there and find out what kind of trouble she was in."

Alabama hopped on the desk.

Her skirt rode up.

Her legs dangled.

She leaned back, studied Wilde and said, "Do you want my opinion?"

"No."

"Good, because here it is," she said. "You need to cut her loose."

"Why?"

"Besides the fact she isn't a paying case?"

Wilde grunted.

That part was true.

Financially the whole thing was a Moby Dick sized negative. Negatives didn't pay the rent. Negatives kicked you to the curb and stomped on your head.

He blew smoke.

"Look," he said. "Someone needs to tie it up. Fingers isn't going to do it. So if not me, then who?"

"But—"

"I'm the one who sent her into the alley."

"Don't try to trick me Wilde," Alabama said. "You're in love with a dead woman. That's what's going on here."

"That's crazy."

Alabama shook her head.

"It's not healthy, Wilde," she said. "Maybe it feels good but it's not healthy. Just let the whole thing go."

Wilde walked to the window. Down below, Larimer Street buzzed, not like a well-oiled machine, more like a squeaky, rusty, ill-designed contraption that might kill you if you got too close to it. The pickup was parked. The Fedora was still in the back.

"Caught a break," he said. "I'll be right back."

He bounded down the stairs, made his way to the Fedora and dusted it off.

Suddenly Johnnie Fingers appeared from out of nowhere.

He was the same size as Wilde, that or possibly a tad bigger. Under the man's suit was a muscled body that moved like a leopard. He got his face close to Wilde's, clearly not in a good mood, and said, "I'm here about the woman you saw when you were driving away."

"I don't know what you're talking about."

Fingers wasn't impressed.

He hardened his face and said, "Let me be absolutely, one hundred percent clear about something. If a single hair on her head ends up messed up, I'll rip off your head and piss in the hole. There won't be a place on this earth far enough that you can run to it."

He turned.

Then he was gone.

Halfway up the street he spotted Blondie at the curb and kicked the fender as he passed.

Wilde lit a book of matches on fire then a cigarette from that.

He took a deep drag.

It quieted the shaking in his hands but not completely.

6

August 6
Tuesday Afternoon

Back at the office Alabama hardly looked up from her magazine as Wilde told her about how Fingers jumped down his throat. Five minutes later though, she closed the pages and said, "I think I might have a theory."

Wilde lit a cigarette and headed for the door.

"I don't have time," he said. "I'm going to go check Sudden Dance's hotel room."

"Just hear me out, first."

He paused and looked at his watch.

"Ten seconds—"

"Okay. Fingers said he was talking about the woman you saw when you were driving away, right?"

"Right but I wasn't driving away. I already told him that. I came out and the car was gone. It was gone and Sudden Dance was gone."

"Yeah, I appreciate that's what you told him," Alabama said. "He doesn't believe you though."

Wilde frowned.

"That's his problem."

"Wilde, focus," Alabama said. "I think he doesn't believe you because there was a witness as to what happened in the alley. That's the only thing that fits."

Wilde blew smoke.

"That doesn't fit at all," he said. "If there was a witness, then Fingers would know not to focus on me. He'd focus on the person the witness saw."

Alabama walked over to the fan.

She tilted it up, stood over it and let the breeze blow up her legs.

"The alley was dark," she said. "Pretend you're someone walking down the sidewalk and you happen to look into the alley. You see two people in a scuffle, a man and a woman. They're fighting about something. Maybe the man is trying to come onto her and she's fighting him off. The thing is, you see something happening. Then the man pulls out a knife and stabs her in the gut. She drops to the ground and he stabs her again in the chest."

Wilde leaned against the door, picturing it.

"Go on."

"It's dark in the alley," she said. "You can tell it's a man doing the attack. He's wearing a suit. He has a hat on. But it's too dark for you to see his face."

Wilde sucked on the words.

They felt like a disease in his lungs.

"He throws her into the car to take her somewhere and dump her," she said. "Now he's barreling up the alley towards the street with the headlights on. He's coming straight at you. You're like a deer, frozen, staring with disbelief at the lights. At the last second you jump out of the way. He squeals around the corner and keeps going. But he got a good look at you, a real good look."

Wilde exhaled.

"That's a pretty complicated story," he said.

"Not really," Alabama said. "At first, she doesn't want to make a police report. She really won't be much help because she never saw the man's face. Plus she doesn't want her name in the file. She's afraid the killer will get it. She's afraid he'll think that she saw more than she really did."

"Then how would Fingers know about her if she never made a report?"

"Because she changed her mind and decided to do her civic duty, or maybe she just made an anonymous call," Alabama said. "Either way, Fingers now has a description of a man who may well be you, but it's not solid enough for him to arrest you yet. So what he does is give you a warning to not even think about harming the woman you saw as you pulled out of the alley. He doesn't care about the Indian but he does care about this other girl, the witness."

It made sense.

It made dangerous, ugly sense.

"I just had a bad thought," Wilde said.

"Which is what?"

"Which is, the dead woman in the well could be the witness on the sidewalk."

"If that's the case you better not get associated with her."

"You mean don't tell Fingers?"

"That's exactly what I mean," Alabama said.

Wilde paced next to the windows, framing scenarios and running them to their logical conclusions.

"Maybe I spoke too fast," he said. "The timing doesn't fit. The woman in the well has been dead for at least a couple of days. When I talked to Fingers this morning, he could care less about the case. He didn't know anything about a witness. That's something he found out after I left, within the last couple of hours."

"Maybe yes, maybe no," Alabama said.

"Meaning what?"

"Meaning maybe he was just playing dumb this morning. Maybe he was just trying to give you enough rope to hang yourself."

Wilde mashed the butt in the ashtray.

"I'll be back in an hour or two."

Then he was gone.

7

August 6
Tuesday Afternoon

Chasing a long-shot, Wilde went to the Kenmark, where Sudden Dance was still technically checked in. The man behind the desk was a mean-looking guy Wilde had never seen before. Whether he would hand over the room key for a couple of bucks and a lame story was problematic. If this were the Metropolitan, the fleabag to end all fleabags, the answer would be easy. Anyone there on either side of the desk would do anything for a buck. But the Kenmark wasn't the Met. The Kenmark kept her legs together. Wilde gave the mean guy one last look, didn't like what he saw, and then hoofed it around to the back alley where he silently climbed the fire escape and accessed the room—207—through a window.

There, he was in.

The bed was unmade.

She sheets were down and the pillow was crooked.

The bathroom door was open. On the sink were the usual suspects—a toothbrush, hairbrush, half-used soap and the like. The hairbrush had a few long, black strands in it. Water spots marked the counter and the mirror.

On the dresser, next to a pair of white sunglasses, was a suitcase. Inside were clothes, some fancy and some comfortable. A few longer garments hung in the closet.

The room looked like it belonged to a woman who had gotten all dolled up for a Saturday night on the town and then never came back.

Wilde opened the door and checked the outside knob.

As he expected, a *Do Not Disturb* sign hung on it.

He closed it tight and made sure it was locked.

The room had no secrets.

Whatever trouble Sudden Dance had been in, the room didn't know.

Wilde lit a smoke, laid down on the bed and stared at the ceiling. Usually he knew what his next play would be. This time he didn't. He didn't know where to look next, who to talk to next, what to think next or where to go next. Everywhere he looked, all he saw was dead end, dead end and more dead end.

Maybe Alabama was right.

Maybe he needed to cut the whole thing loose and

get back to real clients who had real problems and showed their appreciation with real money.

He took a long drag and blew a ring.

On reflection, maybe he was wrong about the dead woman in the well. Maybe she wasn't the witness. Maybe she was someone who was driving down the road and came across the killer when he was broken down out there in the middle of the night.

Maybe she stopped to help.

Footsteps and talking mouths came down the hallway. Wilde held his breath and listened. It could be Johnnie Fingers coming to take a look at the dead woman's place, trying to find evidence to bring Wilde down.

The voices came right up to the door and then just as quickly swept past.

Wilde needed to get out of there.

He sat up and in the process detected something weird about the mattress, almost as if there was something hard in it. He checked under the blanket and found nothing. Then he set the half-gone smoke in an ashtray and pulled the mattress up. Under it, tied to the bottom of the bed frame, was a thin briefcase. What he'd felt were the knots of the rope pressing against the underside of the mattress. The briefcase was positioned so that if anyone looked under the bed they wouldn't see it, at least not unless they got their head right on the floor and then tilted their eyes up diagonally.

He slid the case out of the rope and set it on the bed.

It was locked.

The key wasn't on the dresser or anywhere else in sight. It was probably in Sudden Dance's purse.

It had something to do with the trouble the woman was in. Whatever was inside might even be the reason she was killed.

Suddenly voices came down the hallway.

Wilde grabbed the briefcase and made his way out the window. A glance back showed the door opening and a man and a woman already entering.

Wilde ducked down before anyone turned their eyes.

There was no time to shut the window.

He knew the man.

He was a private investigator by the name of Nicholas Dent, not one of Wilde's favorite people in the world; not just because the man was an asshole, which he was, but because he didn't serve in the war, ostensibly because of some kind of medical condition, asthma or some such nonsense. As far as Wilde was concerned, there wasn't enough time in the day to worry about the guys who didn't step up when the stepping was needed.

The woman was his secretary, Janet.

Wilde stayed low, made his way down the fire escape and vanished up the alley with the briefcase in hand.

8

August 6
Tuesday Afternoon

Back at the office Wilde tossed his hat at the rack, got a ringer, and kept the shock off his face as walked to the desk and set the briefcase on top. Alabama ignored the hat and concentrated on the mystery item.

"What's in there?"

"Probably my obituary. Do the honors and get it open, will you? You'll have to force it, it's locked."

She got it open with a pair of scissors.

Inside was money, a lot of money, tens and twenties and fives and ones, all jammed in.

Alabama gave Wilde a look.

"What'd you do, rob a bank?"

Wilde set a book of matches on fire, lit a smoke, filled 'Bama in and said, "Count it. I want to know how much a life is worth."

"You think this is why Sudden Dance got murdered?"

He nodded.

"I'm sure of it. Too bad for the asshole that he killed her for nothing."

Alabama divided the bills into piles.

It was adding up fast but that's not what interested Wilde. What interested him was that underneath it all was a photo of Sudden Dance with another woman, obviously friends, both happy and smiling for the camera. No inscription, date or writing was on the back. The other woman, a blond, was similar in age to Sudden Dance, in her early to mid-twenties, and equally attractive. Wilde showed the photo to Alabama and said, "She had a friend."

"Or an enemy," she said.

Wilde blew smoke.

"They look like friends to me."

"Yeah, well, enemies are nothing more than friends that you apply time to," she said. "Maybe the friend is the one who killed her."

Wilde tried to picture it.

The picture wouldn't come into focus.

"Either way, it's something," he said.

"Everything's something," Alabama said. "I can't believe how much money this is. It's already over three grand."

"Keep counting."

She set a five to the side and tapped her finger

on it.

"That's for a new dress," she said. "Don't even think about touching it."

He smiled.

"Fair enough."

The photograph was taken outside in early evening. The women were standing in front of a building, one they might have just come out of. They looked a little drunk and had their arms around each other's waist. Wilde didn't recognize the building but was pretty sure it wasn't from Denver. The color was wrong for Denver. It could be a bar or a hotel.

He put the photo in his wallet, tossed the old butt out the window and lit a new one.

"I can't figure out what that sleaze Dent was doing at the room," he said.

"He was probably after the money."

"Yeah but how would he know about it?"

Alabama gave him a look.

"You're making me lose count, Bryson. Stop talking."

"Yes ma'am."

Outside Larimer Street scurried and buzzed and tangoed to its own twisted little beat. Suddenly Wilde remembered something, something bad, something that made his temples tighten; namely that when he lifted the mattress up back at the Kenmark, he set his cigarette on the edge of the ashtray. He never went back for it after finding the briefcase. It would have still been there, still burning, when Dent came into the room.

Dent would have been smart enough to look out the window.

He knew Wilde.

True, Wilde never turned around, but Dent might have recognized him from behind. He would have seen Wilde making off with a briefcase.

"I think I messed up," he said.

"Quiet. I'm counting."

The final count came up to $5,231.

"That's half a house," Alabama said. "What are you going to do with your share?"

"My share?"

She ran a finger down his chest.

"What'd you think, that I was going to keep it all? You're entitled to some of it; I'd say, oh, I don't know, twenty-five percent or thereabouts."

"You're so generous."

9

August 6
Tuesday Afternoon

Wilde couldn't get the body at the bottom of the well out of his head. Somewhere out there in the world people were aching, not knowing where she was. She deserved to be out of there, away from the spiders and the grime and the pathetic insult of it all. She wasn't a chunk of trash to be thrown away. She deserved to be properly buried and mourned. She deserved justice, too. Wilde lit a smoke, turned on the radio and twisted the dial until he got a tolerable song, *T-99 Blues,* one of Jimmy Nelsen's better efforts.

Then he pulled a map out of the bottom drawer, showed Alabama the location of the well and had her place a call to police headquarters. She ended up getting connected to Johnnie Fingers. She told him she was out exploring the country earlier today with a friend. They came across an old well. It looked like there was a woman's dead body at the bottom.

"We dropped some stones on her and she didn't move," Alabama said. "I think she's dead."

Fingers grunted.

"That's a long ways from Denver."

"I know but she could be from here. Maybe someone from here is missing and that's where she ended up."

"What'd you say your name was again?"

"Jane," she said.

"Jane what?"

"Jane Jones," she said. "Someone should check that well out. That's all I'm calling about."

She hung up and looked at Wilde.

He blew smoke with approval.

"Good job."

"Do you think he'll follow up?"

Wilde nodded.

"Oh yeah, he'll check it out," he said. "He's already thinking it's Sudden Dance. Once he finds her he can nail me. That's his ultimate goal."

T-99 Blues ended.

Call Operator 210 took its place.

Wilde let it play.

"If the woman in the well is the witness, Fingers will make a beeline straight for me," Wilde said. "If he isn't knocking on the door by tomorrow, that means the body isn't the witness. That means that the witness is still alive; still alive and in serious danger, to be precise."

Alabama punched him on the arm.

"Don't tell me you're going to go running off on a wild goose chase to save her," she said.

He tapped ashes out the window and sat on the ledge.

"If someone tries to kill her it will be the same person who killed Sudden Dance," Wilde said. "She's our best connection to the guy. Our only connection, actually."

"Wilde, let it go."

"We need to find out her name," he said.

"How?"

"I don't know. All I know is that we need to. We also need to figure out what that sleaze-bucket Nicholas Dent has to do with all this. Why was he in Sudden Dance's hotel room? That's what I want to know—"

Alabama tilted her head.

"If you really want to know, we can pay a visit to his office tonight," she said. "He should have a file, right?"

Wilde smiled.

Dent was dumb.

He always had to write everything down.

Whatever he was up to, it would be there on paper in good old No. 2.

"Good idea," he said.

"Really?"

"Yes."

"We're really going to do it?"

He nodded.

"We just need to be damn sure we don't get caught. I'm actually wondering if Dent and Fingers are somehow in some kind of cahoots with each other."

"Wow, now there's a strange thought."

"I've had stranger," Wilde said.

"Maybe but they all involved sex. This one doesn't involve sex, does it?"

He smiled.

"You're too much."

Wilde turned his attention to the money, the money on the desk still piled in denominations, the beautiful and very tempting $5,231.

"You're thinking what to buy me," Alabama said. "Start with lingerie." She grabbed his hand and put it on her heart. "Feel that, you're already getting me excited."

He pulled his hand away.

"'Bama, get serious. This isn't ours."

"Sure it is."

Wilde struck a book of matches. The pungent odor of sulfur filled and air and gray smoke snaked towards the ceiling. He let it burn for a second, lit a cigarette and tossed the flames out the window.

"You're going to burn down Denver," Alabama

said.

"Worst things have happened. My guess is that Sudden Dance stole the money. That's what got her killed. The money is our second best connection to the killer, after the witness, assuming she's still alive. The money is our bait."

"Bait isn't bait unless the rat knows about it," Alabama said. "What we need to do is start flashing it around so he knows we have it. We'll start with that lingerie I was talking about."

Wilde took a deep drag.

"Actually, you might be onto something," he said.

"Lingerie?" She ran a finger down his chest. "You're picturing me in it, aren't you?"

"No."

"No?"

"No, not that much."

"But some—"

"Maybe a little but only because you're making me," he said. "The flashing is a good idea. We'll flash the briefcase though, not the money. The briefcase is pretty unique." That was true. It was unusually thin, with tanned leather faded by wear and scuffed at the corners, with oversized black latches. "For right now we'll stash the money someplace safe and keep our hands off it. And when I say *our hands*, I'm talking about the things at the end of your arms."

She held them up and wiggled her fingers.

"These," she said.

He nodded.

"Precisely."

10

August 6
Tuesday Night

Even though he was a sleaze-bag, or maybe because of it, Nicholas Dent got a lot of secret work from the local uppity-ups and correspondingly had an office that was a lot better than Wilde's. It was a standalone structure of considerable size on Sherman, a stone's throw from the guts of the financial district where the best-paying clients in Denver spent their working hours and hid their secret affairs and indiscretions. Once an ornate mansion, now the place housed only sleaze.

After dark Tuesday night, Wilde drove past that palace of sleaze with Alabama in the passenger seat.

The windows were black.

No lights came from inside.

"The pace is dead," Alabama said.

Wilde agreed.

They parked on 16th, hoofed it back through the alley and found all the lower windows locked. Alabama pointed to an upper one and said, "That one's half open."

"It's too high."

Alabama spotted a rusty 55-gallon drum in the weeds and said, "Help me roll that over here."

"Why?"

"We're going to get on it and then I'm going to climb up you until I'm standing on your shoulders and then I'm going to grab the ledge of the window and pull myself in."

"That's not doable."

"Sure it is," she said. "I don't want you looking up my skirt though."

Two minutes later Alabama was up and in.

She lifted up her skirt, stuck her behind out the window and wiggled it. Then she looked down at Wilde looking up and said, "Hey, you're not supposed to be doing that."

Then she disappeared.

Thirty seconds later the back door opened and Wilde was in.

Dent's primary office was on the lower level at the back. Wilde pulled the window coverings shut and powered up a flashlight.

He expected a mess.

That's not what he got.

Everything was clean and organized.

A number of files were on the desk, each neatly labeled in thick black writing. None said *Sudden Dance* or *Saturday Murder* or *Bryson Wilde* or *Johnnie Fingers* or anything else of interest.

"Check the file cabinets," he said.

Alabama obliged.

One of the files on the desk was labeled *Nicole Fountain.* Inside were several pages of lined yellow paper with pencil notes.

"Bingo."

"You got something?"

"Yeah, I think so."

"Let's see."

Page after page Wilde read, handing each one to Alabama when he was done. The story that emerged was so detailed that it seemed as if Wilde was right there.

* * *

A woman named Nicole Fountain phoned Dent's home number Sunday morning wanting to meet with him as soon as possible, before Monday if possible. They met at the office an hour later.

"I'm a waitress at the Down Towner so I don't have much money," she said. "If this is going to cost a lot, I'll pay you but it will have to be spread out a little here and there."

"This meeting is free," Dent said. "Don't worry about money for the moment and just tell me what's going on."

She composed her thoughts.

"Okay," she said, "Saturday night me and a couple of girlfriends went to a club called the Bokoray. The band was from out of town but the guy who was drumming was a local guy named Bryson Wilde. I don't know him personally but I see him at the clubs now and then. We've never talked or anything like that but like I said I've see him around."

Dent tapped two cigarettes out of a pack and extended one to Nicole who waved it off.

"No, thanks."

Dent lit his and blew a ring.

"I know Wilde."

"I figured that," she said. "Anyway, during the breaks he was getting all cozy with a woman in a white dress. She was extremely pretty, almost like a model or something."

"Sounds like his type."

"She was getting drunker and drunker as the night went on."

"Sounds even more like his type."

"She was standing by the wall. Lots of guys went over to her but she brushed them off. She only had eyes for Wilde."

"Lucky him."

"Right," she said. "Anyway, the night ended. I

used the little girl's room before I left and then headed for the car where my friends were waiting for me.
I was walking down the sidewalk and just happened
to look down the alley. I saw a woman and a man in
some kind of altercation—it was the woman from
the club, the one in the white dress. The man had the
woman by the hair and was yelling at her and she was
yelling back. Then all of a sudden the man had knife
in his hand, a really big one, and he stabbed her in
the gut two or three times, real violently, almost as if
he was trying to push the blade all the way through
her body. She crumpled like a doll and fell down into
the dirt. He stabbed her again, this time in the chest,
two times. Then he pulled her body up, threw it in
the passenger seat and took off. At that point he was
coming right at me. I was like a deer in headlights,
totally frozen. At the last second I somehow got my
wits and jumped out of the way. The car squealed
around the corner to the right and disappeared down
the street." She held her hand out. "Look, my hand
is shaking."

Dent held it steady.

"Was the man Wilde?"

"That's my assumption but I have to be honest, I
can't say for certain," she said. "It was too dark when
he was back in the alley. Then when he came at me,
all I could see was the headlights. They were blinding.
They were like two suns shooting at me."

"So Wilde got a good look at you and knows

you're a witness," Dent said. "That's what this comes down to."

She nodded.

"Right, except like I said, I can't swear it was Wilde. To tell you the truth, he never struck me as that kind of guy."

Dent grunted.

"A guy who's not that kind of guy can turn into that kind of guy if he's drunk and the woman he thinks he's going to end up with in bed suddenly changes her mind. That's how devils get made and trust me, they get made every day." He tapped ashes into the tray. "So what exactly do you want from me?"

Her eyes darted.

"My natural instinct was to file a police report," she said. "The more I thought about it though, the more I didn't want my name involved. I was worried that it would make its way to the killer. That might not be a problem if Wilde was the killer, but it might be a big problem if someone else was. Also, I never got a look at the guy, so I don't know if I have all that much useful information to tell when you get right down to it." She hesitated and then added, "What I want you to do is find out what's going on. Find out who the woman is. Find out who the killer is. Figure out how much trouble I'm in for seeing what I did. The answers are important because if I'm in real trouble then I'm going to get out of Denver. I don't want to do that if I don't have to because I really don't have anywhere else to go. I don't have any family or anything."

Dent blew smoke.

"My advice is to make a police report," he said. "I'll go with you. Before we go, I'll make a call and get an absolute guarantee that your name won't be put in the file or ever mentioned to anyone."

The woman's hands shook.

"I'll think about it."

"You do that," Dent said. "In the meantime I'll sniff around a little, on the house."

"Are you serious?"

"Sure, why not?"

DAY

FIVE

August 7
Wednesday

11

August 7
Wednesday Morning

Wednesday morning Wilde had one thought and one thought only, namely to find out if the witness, Nicole Fountain, was alive or whether she was the body at the bottom of the well. To that effect, he headed to the Down Towner where the woman supposedly waitressed.

With Sudden Dance's briefcase in hand, he made two passes by the windows but got no results.

He couldn't see inside that good.

Just inside the door was a cigarette machine. He made sure he had correct change, entered, set the briefcase down and slipped coins in the slot, ostensibly paying no attention to anything else, just one more guy out of smokes and now getting them so he didn't turn into a big green lizard or some such thing. The pack fell to the chute. He scooped it up, tapped a stick out and lit it with a match as his eyes took a quick sweep around the room.

Across the way a strawberry-haired waitress was pouring coffee at a booth.

Her back was to him.

When she headed for the counter her profile came into view. She was in her mid-twenties with a curvy body and an easy smile. Her lips were ruby-red. A cigarette dangled from them. Wilde recognized her from around town. She'd been at the club Saturday night with a couple of friends.

He opened the door to leave.

As he took one last look, something happened that he didn't expect.

The woman was staring directly at him.

Her smile was gone.

Her eyes were serious.

Wilde's grip tightened on the briefcase.

He took one last look.

Then he was gone.

At the office Alabama pulled no punches. "You do a lot of things that aren't exactly brilliant," she said, "but I'm going to put that one right up there at the top."

"Why?"

"Because she's going to think you're stalking her."

Wilde blew smoke.

"I barely looked at her."

"That's not the point," she said. "The point is that she saw you kill someone Saturday night. She was in your headlights when you pulled out. Now here you are on Tuesday morning showing up where she works, pretending not to look at her when you really were. Just a weird coincidence? I think not—"

Wilde looked out the window.

"Some day I want to wake up and be one of those saps out there," he said. "I just want to wander around aimlessly and not care about anything except getting wine in my gut."

Alabama rolled her eyes.

"Look," she said, "you know you didn't kill anyone and you think that's some kind of magical trump card that you can just pull out and wave up in the air whenever you want and then everything will be just fine. You better think again because I have news for you, truth is a second-class citizen."

Wilde wrinkled his brow.

"Like being an Indian," he said.

Alabama came over, put his arms around him and laid her head on his chest.

"You need to worry about Fingers," she said. "Especially if Nicole Fountain tells him you were at her work this morning. Fingers shot a guy last year. Did you know that?"

The words rolled up a memory but it was faint.

"Remind me again."

"He shot a guy while he was arresting him," Alabama said. "He shot him cold dead, four times. He thought the guy was a killer. Later it turned out that the guy had an alibi. That didn't help him much though after he was dead."

Wilde tapped his fingers.

"I'm not worried about Fingers. I am, however, worried about Nicole Fountain. My guess is that she's pretty safe during the day. It's the night she has to worry about. Do me a favor and find out where she lives. We'll be staking her out tonight."

Alabama punched his arm.

"Do you even listen to anything I say?"

He put a surprised look on his face.

"I'm sorry," he said. "Have you been talking?"

Two hours later Johnnie Fingers opened the door and walked into the room with an attitude. He nodded at Alabama, focused hard on Wilde and said, "There's a rumor going around that you were out taking a stroll this morning."

Wilde tapped two cigarettes out of a pack and extended one to Fingers.

He knew what this was about.

It wouldn't be pretty.

Fingers hesitated and then accepted.

Wilde set a book of matches on fire, lit them up and said, "I thought strolling was legal."

"It is," Fingers said. "It can be dangerous though. Sometimes people got out for a stroll and get blindsided by an ice truck. Squish, squash. Taking a stroll in the wrong place can be dangerous, even deadly."

Wilde blew smoke.

"Is that why you're here? To warn me about ice trucks?"

Fingers shook his head.

He reached into his pocket, pulled out a photo and tossed it on the desk. It depicted a young woman in her mid-twenties, lying dead at the bottom of a well.

"Is that your Indian friend?"

"No. You can tell she's not Indian."

"True. Do you know her?"

"No."

"Are you sure?"

"Yes," Wilde said. "I've never seen her before."

Fingers cast an eye on Alabama.

"What's your name, pretty lady?"

"Alabama."

"Do you work for this guy?"

She nodded.

"Did you know he was in the war?"

"Yes."

"He was gunner in a B-17G Flying Fortress, which was a bomber that had four Wright supercharged Radial engines with a real distinctive growl. You could hear them two countries away. He sat back there in that little glass bubble at the bottom of the plane with his hands on the trigger of a 50-caliber machine gun."

Wilde grunted.

"You've been doing your homework."

"No, it's common knowledge. Me myself, I could never do anything like that. Flying scares the crap out of me even when people aren't shooting at you. I wouldn't be worried so much about a shot coming through the glass and taking me out. What I'd be worried about is a shot taking out the glass and then the sky sucking me out. Can you imagine falling from up there, still alive, with the ground coming up at you faster and faster?"

Wilde tapped ashes.

"You're strapped in," he said. "That would never happen."

"Well, that's good." To Alabama he said, "What'd you do during the war?"

"What's it matter?"

"I was just curious. You did something. I can tell. What was it? Did you sew uniforms or something?"

"No."

Fingers put disagreement on his face. "Come on, you did something."

"I was ten," she said. "I spent my time worrying about my father."

"He was in the war?"

She nodded.

"He got killed in the Philippines."

Fingers frowned.

"I'm sorry to hear that."

Alabama's eyes moistened. The sight sent bark and bite into Wilde's brain and he trained it on Fingers.

"I think your visit here is done," he said.

"Sure," Fingers said. "The woman in the photo, by the way, we don't know who she is yet, but we found her out in the country, not too far from where your car was," Fingers said. "Pretty strange, huh?"

Wilde took a deep drag.

"What are you getting at?"

"Nothing," Fingers said. "I just thought maybe you could help me. Do you have any idea why she'd be out there dead, not too far from where your car was?"

Wilde looked out the window and then at Fingers.

"When my car got a flat, whoever it was that took Sudden Dance had to get out of there somehow. Maybe this woman saw the car broken down and stopped to help. Maybe she ended up dead for her kindness."

Fingers nodded.

"That's the same theory I came up with. I'm really impressed that it rolled right off your tongue. For me, I had to mull it over for hours before it came out."

Wilde walked to the door and opened it.

"Have a nice day," he said.

Fingers cast an eye on the briefcase and said, "Nice briefcase."

Then he was gone.

As soon as the man left Alabama said, "He was getting me to talk on purpose. He was trying to figure out if I was the person who called and ended up talking to him about the woman in the well. I'm sure he recognized my voice. Now he's going to have you connected to that body."

Wilde nodded.

"I know."

"What I don't get is why was he talking about you being in a bomber? Was that just to lead over to me and have a reason to ask what I did?"

Wilde blew smoke.

"I think he was giving me a warning," Wilde said. "It's his way of saying he's holding off for the time being on taking me down, because we were both in the war."

"You think?"

He nodded.

"It's his way of saying he gave me a break."

"But now it's gone?"

"Right, now it's gone."

A good song came on the radio, *Lawdy Miss Clawdy* by Lloyd Price. Alabama turned it up and said, "The dead woman in the photo that Fingers showed us, I've seen her around somewhere."

Wilde raised an eyebrow.

"Where?"

"I'm trying to think—"

Wilde waited.

Seconds passed, then more.

Alabama's face brightened.

"Got it," she said.

"Good, where?"

She threw a look his way. "First say, Alabama you're so pretty." Wilde scrunched his face and then complied. "Nice of you to notice," Alabama said. "I've seen her down by the Daniels & Fisher Tower. She was all dressed up real fancy; not like a whore, more like someone important."

"Someone important, huh?"

"Yeah. She looked expensive."

Wilde set a book of matches on fire.

"Alabama, you're so pretty," he said.

She smiled.

"Nice of you to notice."

"Come on, we have work to do."

12

August 7
Wednesday Afternoon

Wilde's veins were beginning to fill with more and more lightning. He'd always pictured the body from the well as belonging to someone who lived in the rural area. Now it turns out she was probably from Denver and that one simple fact turned everything on its head and shook it so hard that every ounce of spare change fell out of the pockets. If the woman wasn't just an innocent driver who stopped at the MG after it broke down, then how did she end up out there?

Plus, she was *expensive*.

She was somebody.

More importantly, she had to be somehow connected to Sudden Dance. It was too much of a coincidence that both women ended up in the same dark deadly corner of the universe at the same time without there being some type of connection between them.

Maybe their only connection was that the same man killed both of them.

But then again, maybe it was something deeper and more complex, something with a plan or a history to it.

Wilde knew the Daniels & Fisher Tower well.

It was the highest building between the Mississippi and San Francisco, situated smack in the center of the matter on the city's main downtown drag, 16th Street. At the top was a clock tower. Wilde had been up there on more than one occasion with a bottle of wine and a member of the softer persuasion. From there, the city lights stretched to infinity in all directions.

Right now Wilde and Alabama were at the foot of the building next to the revolving door.

Bodies went in, bodies came out.

In Wilde's left hand was Sudden Dance's briefcase, the bait, if anyone was interested enough to spot it.

He set it on the sidewalk, lit a smoke and tossed the match to the ground.

"The more I think about it, the more you shouldn't be here," he told Alabama. "This whole thing is getting too damned dicey."

She wasn't impressed.

"Be nice," she said. "Remember, you're going to

need someone to bail you out of jail."

He took a deep drag.

"Stay here, I'll be right back."

He disappeared into the revolving doors and headed across the lobby to a reception desk. Behind it a woman with a babushka-covered bun gave him a hard look. Wilde set the briefcase on the counter, smiled and said, "I'm in a bit of a predicament."

The woman relaxed her face.

"Why? What's wrong?"

Wilde tapped his fingers on the briefcase.

"I was supposed to deliver this briefcase to someone this morning outside on the sidewalk," he said. "I got here late. Here's the bad part. The woman works in this building but I forgot her name."

"Did you write it down?"

"I did but it's at home," he said. "Here's what she looks like. She dresses real nice, very expensive, if you know what I mean. She's in her mid-twenties and pretty, with blond hair."

The woman retreated in thought.

Then her face brightened.

"Are you talking about Alley London?"

Wilde nodded.

"Right. That's her."

"I haven't seen here come in yet," the woman said. "Come to think of it, I haven't seen her in a couple of days."

"What floor is she on?"

"Eight."

Wilde smiled his best smile and said, "You're a peach." Ten seconds later he was in the stairwell climbing up to eight with a beat in his chest.

The stairwell dumped him into a hallway that had a number of doors, the most interesting of which was the one on the prime side, where the offices had views of both the jags of the Rockies fifteen miles to the west and the bustle of 16th Street down below. That half of the floor, the sweet half, belonged to Banders & Rock, Attorneys-At-Law.

Wilde opened the door and immediately got dumped into a receptionist who, by the expression on her face, didn't mind the way he looked, not at all.

He smiled and said, "I'm here to see Alley London."

The woman frowned.

"She's out this week. Can someone else in the office help you?"

Wilde shook his head.

"No, I can wait. When will she be back in?"

"Monday."

"That's fine. I'll come back Monday."

At street level Alabama had a somber expression. "Fingers is on our tail," she said. "He's been ducking in and out of sight ever since we got here. I've been busy trying to not stare directly at him. It hasn't been

easy. Right now he's over there on the sidewalk behind that red pickup."

Wilde set the briefcase on the sidewalk, lit a cigarette and purposely pointed his face in the non-Fin-
gers direction.

"We need to lose him," he said. "The woman from
the well is someone named Alley London. We need to
find out where she lives and get into her house and
figure out why she ended up dead in a well and, more
importantly, how she's connected to Sudden Dance."

"If at all—"

"Right, if at all. She's a lawyer with Banders &
Rock, by the way. They're some fancy law firm up on
the 8th floor. That's why she looked expensive."

"Unlike you and me who aren't making any money. How'd you find that out all that without a picture
of her?"

He blew smoke.

"I smiled," he said.

"You know how to smile?"

"Yeah, I learned last week." He took a drag and
added, "The firm doesn't know she's dead yet."

"That's weird."

He shrugged.

"She out this week so no one's missing her when
she doesn't show up."

"Out doing what?"

"I don't know," he said. "I have half a mind to turn
around and wave at Fingers." The smoke was down

to Wilde's fingers. He took one last draw, flicked it into the street and said, "Let's go."

According to the phone book, the body from the well, Alley London, lived just south of downtown, a block off Broadway. Wilde zigzagged Blondie through the city until he was sure no one was on his tail and then made his way to the woman's street, parking three doors down under an Elm.

"Stay here," he said.

Alabama got out and said, "Apparently this is one of those days when I'm not listening very well."

Wilde lit a smoke and gauged whether he would lose if he argued.

He would.

"Apparently not," he said.

The house was a small bungalow awash in a sea of the same. It was locked tight with no clean way in. Wilde broke the back door glass with an elbow, setting off a violent and non-stop bark from a dog behind a fence.

It didn't matter.

They were already in.

Wilde half-expected the placed to be trashed by someone looking for something.

It wasn't.

There were no signs of searching.

There were no signs of a struggle.

On the kitchen counter was a bowl of fruit, still

fresh enough to eat. In the bathroom, several pairs of stockings hung over the shower rod, long since dried to perfection. An ashtray next to the couch in the living room was packed with butts. On closer inspection, lots had lipstick but lots didn't, possibly the earmarks of a man. Wilde squashed his butt on top of it all and lit a new one.

"So what are we looking for exactly?"

"Anything that shows she knew Sudden Dance," he said. "That's the big one. Or who else did she know? Who had a motive to kill her? I also want to figure out if she had a car or not and if so whether it's parked around here somewhere or whether it's missing."

"Whoa," Alabama said. "Look at this."

This was a piece of paper.

Handwritten on it were the words, *Bryson Wilde.* Directly below those words was his office phone number, written in the same feminine script. Nothing else was on the paper, only his name and number.

"What's this about?" Alabama said.

"I don't know."

"Did she call you?"

"Not that I remember."

"Think."

"I am. No, I never talked to her." He focused on her. "How about you?"

Her eyes faded and then returned.

"Maybe."

"Maybe."

"Someone called last week when you were out. It was a woman but she never left her name."

"What did she want?"

"She didn't say."

"Did she say she'd call back?"

"No, she asked for you, I said you weren't in at the moment and she asked when you'd be back. I told her probably in an hour or two. She said thanks and hung up."

"How'd she sound?"

"I don't follow—"

"Did she sound like someone was out to kill her or whether she was looking for protection or something like that?"

Alabama wrinkled her forehead.

"Not that I remember," she said. "Actually her voice was sort of soft, almost like she was whispering."

"Like she didn't want someone to overhear her?"

"Possibly."

The paper was fancy, off-white and thicker than most, with a watermark. It had been folded. No others like it were visible. "This is from her work," he said. "She wrote my name and number down while she was at work, folded it up and stuck it in her purse." He shoved it in his wallet next to the photo of Sudden Dance and said, "Good thing we got here before Fingers did. This is a one-way ticket to jail.

Keep looking around."

They found a black-and-white photo of Alley sitting behind the wheel of parked car. Her arm hung out the window. A cigarette dangled from her hand. A mischievous smile graced her face. It was a summer day.

She was happy.

The sun caught the edge of her face.

Her hair was loose and windblown.

The vehicle was white.

A string of beads hung from the rearview mirror.

13

August 7
Wednesday Afternoon

Outside at Blondie something was off but Wilde couldn't put his finger on what it was. It wasn't until they got back to Larimer Street and he reached into the backseat for Sudden Dance's briefcase that it came to him.

The backseat was empty.

The briefcase was gone.

He said, "Someone ate the bait," then stepped out, closed the door and lit a cigarette as he cast an eye up and down the street.

Alabama looked at him over Blondie's top.

"Fingers?"

Wilde shook his head. "No, we lost Fingers. We lost him good. This isn't the work of Fingers."

"So, the killer then?"

Wilde's face tightened.

Up the street on the opposite side was a man too stationary, a menacing man in a suit that Wilde had never seen before, now lighting a cigarette and leaning a muscular body against a building, his face turning in every direction except towards Wilde.

"Get into the office and lock the door," he said. "The gun is in the drawer. Use it if you have to."

"Wilde—"

"What."

"I'm sorry."

"About what?"

"It's my fault. I didn't lock the car door."

"If you did he would have just busted the window. So actually you did good."

Then he turned and walked up the street with his head down and his eyes on the sidewalk, ostensibly just a guy in thought as he walked, not paying any attention to his surroundings, probably consumed with a dame.

When he got to where the man was, he looked across the street for the first time.

The figure was gone.

He wasn't up.

He wasn't down.

He wasn't anywhere.

Up, that's the way he probably went. That's the way Wilde would have gone. He headed that way, now at a brisk walk and with his eyes high.

Come on.

Don't be afraid.

You want the money.

Come and get it.

It's all yours.

At the corner of 14th he looked to the left.

Bingo!

There he was, half a block ahead and moving fast. Wilde flicked his butt to the gutter and picked up the pace. The gap closed step by step.

"Hey buddy, hold up a minute."

The man turned his head and then stopped. He was bigger than Wilde expected, with a flat-nosed boxer's face and a fancy gold watch on his left wrist.

"Yeah?"

"I know you from someone," Wilde said. "What's your name?"

The man hardened his face.

"No, you don't know me," the man said.

Wilde watched him turn and leave.

Then he lit a smoke and headed back to the office.

There the door wasn't locked like he'd told Alabama to do. She was seated behind the desk with her legs propped up and her skirt pulled up above her knees. Her eyes lifted up from a magazine.

"That was fast," she said.

"I told you—"

She brought something off her lap and set it on the desk. It was the gun.

"So the guy didn't pan out I assume."

Wilde sat on the window ledge.

"I don't know," he said. "I got a close-up look at him. If he shows up again I'll know him. Did you check the money?"

She nodded.

"It's all there except for a twenty that I put in my purse."

Wilde pulled the photo out of his wallet, the one with the lawyer, Alley London, sitting behind the wheel of a white car. Not much of the vehicle was in view but from what was there it looked like a Packard. No white Packards, or white anythings, had been anywhere around the lawyer's house, either in the side yard or on the street.

He tossed the photo on the desk.

"I have a dilemma," he said. "I got this whole bait thing in motion without getting you out of the picture first. Now you're at risk, at least until the guy gets his hands on the money."

Alabama adjusted her body and in the process managed to hike her skirt up to the danger point.

"Don't give up the money, if that's what you're thinking," she said. "Force him to come and get it and then take him down when he does. That was the plan. Keep it the plan."

Wilde tapped ashes out the window.

Across the street was the man, replete with flat nose and the fancy gold wrist, leaning against a building with a smoke dangling from his lips. Wilde pretended not to notice and eased off the ledge.

He motioned over.

"Come here but stay out of sight."

She peeked through the corner of the window.

"That's the guy," Wilde said.

"He looks mean."

"Here's what I want you to do. Sneak out the back way. Head over to the Down Towner and keep an eye on the witness."

"You mean the waitress."

"I mean both," he said. "Nicole Fountain. Don't come back to the office for any reason. I won't be here and I don't want you here alone under any circumstances. Meet me at four o'clock in front of the Daniels & Fisher Tower."

"That's a long time."

"Do some shopping."

She frowned.

"All I have is that twenty—"

He pulled bills from his wallet and forked them over. "Just keep yourself safe until four. Can you do that?"

She ran a finger down his nose.

"I'll buy something sexy."

"I'm serious, 'Bama."

Five minutes later he was in Blondie heading south out of the guts of the city. The top was down. The sun was on his face. On the passenger seat was a shoebox. Inside that shoebox was $5,231, less whatever had stuck to Alabama's fingers. Next to it, also on the seat, was the gun.

The traffic got less congested.

Still, it was too thick to tell if he was being followed.

With any luck he was.

He drove mile after mile after mile.

The buildings got smaller and farther apart and then dropped off altogether as the topography morphed into nature. Magpies took to the air and little yellow butterflies jagged this way and that around prairie bushes. Every once in a while a squashed rattlesnake appeared on the asphalt.

No vehicles were directly behind Wilde.

There was one car, a white one, way back, going the same direction, south, but otherwise not of much interest. It only came into sight on rare occasions when both cars crested.

Still, it could be following even from that far back.

The crossroads were few and were either gravel or dirt.

If Wilde turned down one a rooster-tail would kick up. A tracker would be able to follow.

His chest pounded.

The feeling didn't go away as the miles clicked off. He made it all the way to the well without adventure; the well, the place where Alley London's body got dumped.

He pulled to the side of the road, killed the engine and got out.

The sky was quiet.

The sun was hot.

The air had a soft scent of nature.

Wilde lit a cigarette.

Then he slipped the photo of Alley London under a wiper blade, grabbed the box of money, tucked the gun in his belt and headed up the almost-not-there road that led to the well and the dilapidated structures.

The well was empty now.

Fingers had pulled the body out thanks to Alabama's anonymous report. Other than that the place was exactly as Wilde had left it.

He took a seat in the opening of the house where the front door should be and leaned against the frame.

The shade was an oasis.

Suddenly a horn honked.

He recognized it all too well.

It belonged to Blondie.

Someone was there.

Someone was announcing that he was coming.

He was coming for the money.

He was coming with a brain on fire and murder in his heart.

Wilde tapped a smoke out and lit it.

He had a few minutes.

He might as well use them.

In ten minutes someone would be dead. If it turned out to be the other guy, Wilde would dump his stupid body in the well. The man would take the spot of the woman he killed.

It would be poetic.

14

August 7
Wednesday Afternoon

Wilde set the shoebox on the floor in the middle of the doorway and then took a position behind the shed. Minutes later a man appeared; it was the man from Larimer Street, the one with the flat nose and the expensive gold watch.

In his right hand was a black gun.

He approached cautiously, keeping low, keeping quiet.

Thirty steps away from the structure he stopped.

His eyes fell on the money.

Then he called out, "Wilde!" Wilde's chest pounded at the realization that the man knew his name. "Wilde, all I want is the money. Don't be stupid. I don't want to kill you. There's no reason you have to die. We can do this the civilized way. Do you understand?"

Wilde said nothing.

"The money's not yours," the man said.

Wilde tightened his grip on the gun.

The man stood straight up and lowered his hand.

"My gun's pointed at the ground," he shouted. "Show yourself. I'm not going to shoot."

Wilde stepped out with the gun pointed down.

He was fast.

He was accurate.

He could get the barrel up and a bullet flying before his brain twisted far enough to even know what his body was doing.

"There you are," the man said.

Wilde jerked his arm up, turned to the right and pulled the trigger. The wood next to the money exploded. He fired again and this time the bullet landed where he wanted, on the shoebox, catching the corner and sending it spinning. Bills flew out and twisted wildly in the air before dropping to the ground.

"There's the money. Take it."

The man frowned.

Then he dropped his gun to the ground.

"See?" he said. "No threat here."

Wilde pointed his gun at the man's chest.

His finger tightened on the trigger.

He'd killed men before but most had been from the barrel of a warbird. A nasty image flashed, an image of the man knifing Sudden Dance in the alley, knifing her hard, stabbing her over and over in the gut and then, when she dropped, driving the blade into her heart.

The man took a step towards the money, then another.

"I'll tell you what," he said. "I'll split it with you. Fifty-fifty. That's fair, don't you think? Just put the gun down and cool your heels. We'll work through this. Remember, the money's not yours. You took it."

Wilde didn't listen.

He needed to pull the trigger.

He needed to do it for Sudden Dance.

He needed to do it for Alley London.

The trigger wouldn't pull though.

Then the man pointed at the ground next to Wilde and said, "Rattlesnake."

Wilde turned his head but not much, just enough to verify that it was a trick. What he saw he couldn't believe. Not more than eight feet away a thick brown snake was coming directly at him. The body was brown with wicked spots and the head was a large thick diamond with nasty black eyes. Wilde's eyes went to the tail. The rattle was there, blackish and hard; it wasn't a bull snake.

He shot; once, then again, and again and again, hitting it each time but not squarely until the last pull of the trigger, but hitting it good then, real good, right at the end of the head, hitting it so hard that the head flew off and gooey red guts squirted out of the hole in the body.

He turned back to the boxer to find something he didn't expect.

The man was walking towards him.

"That was six shots," the man said.

His face was hard.

In his hand was a knife.

"That part about not hurting you," the man said, "I'm afraid that was a lie."

Then he charged.

Wilde pulled the trigger.

No response came.

It fell on empty air.

15

August 7
Wednesday Afternoon

It took Wilde a long time to kill the boxer and when it was over his body shut down, collapsing him to the ground on top of the rattlesnake's body, with not enough strength to even roll off. The snake's head was by his head, mere inches away, a foot at most, staring at him out of dead black holes.

He closed his eyes.

The darkness was whiskey.

He was busted; how bad and how far and how deep, he didn't know, but did know it wouldn't be pretty.

It took a long time before he got to his feet.

He would have laid there longer but the sun was chewing him up.

The boxer's eyes were open and eerily shriveled.

The juice was gone.

He looked like a circus freak.

Wilde nudged his face with a foot.

It didn't respond.

He found a wallet in the man's back pocket. It was stuffed with cash, a lot of cash, maybe over a grand. Wilde didn't count it or take it out. He shifted through it for a driver's license or identification papers and found nothing, only the cash. He put the wallet back in the man's pocket, dragged him to the well and dumped him in like the little shit he was. "That's your first step towards hell. Have fun the rest of the way." The bloody knife went in too, thrown in on top of him, plus the gun.

There, that was all of it.

He grabbed the shoebox, gathered the money and got the hell out of there.

Back at Blondie the photo of Alley London had been removed from the windshield wiper and tossed on the ground. Wilde picked it up and stuck it in his wallet.

The boxer's car was parked directly behind Blondie.

Wilde expected it would be Alley's white vehicle. It wasn't; it was an old, blue piece of crap with a temporary tag taped in the rear window. The boxer must have ditched Alley's car somewhere, not needing the risk.

An unopened carton of Camels sat on the seat.

Wilde threw them in Blondie.

The asshole owed him at least that.

The keys were in the ignition.

A plastic dealer's tag was on the ring—Honest Joe's Used Cars. It was a place on upper Colfax. You could buy a car in the front and stolen cigarettes in the back.

Mashed butts were in the ashtray.

Underneath them was a crumpled piece of paper.

Wilde brushed it off and unfolded it.

On it was a handwritten phone number.

He shoved it in his wallet.

Then he got in Blondie, lit a smoke, did a one-eighty and let the miles click off one after another back towards Denver.

He should feel good. The little coward who murdered Sudden Dance was now taking a long, hard dirt nap, killed in the same exact way that he dished it out. Alley London, the poor thing, had her revenge too. Plus the witness, Nicole Fountain, now had nothing to worry about. Still, no smile came to Wilde's face. He was satisfied and wouldn't change an ounce of anything but there was no smile on his face, either on the surface or underneath it.

He sucked the last drag out of a butt and flicked it out the window.

The smoke was magic in his lungs.

Back in Denver he swung by his house for a shower and clothes that weren't ripped to shreds. His body ached in a hundred places but his face was basically intact except for a couple of cuts and a punch of purple under his right eye.

Alabama showed up exactly where and when she was supposed to, namely the D&F Tower at four.

Shopping bags dangled from both hands.

She handed half to Wilde, studied his face and said, "Tell me the other guy looks worse."

He nodded.

"It's over."

"Who was it? That boxer guy?"

"Yes."

"Did you kill him?"

"No, he killed himself when he killed Sudden Dance. But I helped him die."

"Are you going to tell Fingers?"

"No, screw Fingers."

"So does this mean you still have the money?"

"Yes."

"What are we going to do with it?"

"We?"

She ran a finger down his sleeve. "You're going to like what I bought."

"Why, what is it?"

"You'll see. It's skimpy."

At the office something happened that Wilde didn't

expect.

The lock was broken.

The door was ajar.

Inside, the place was trashed to hell and back.

16

Wilde tossed the shoebox of money on the desk, surveyed the mess and said, "Nicholas Dent."

Alabama considered it.

"You think so?"

Wilde set a book of matches on fire and lit a smoke.

"He was looking for the money," he said. "There are only two people in this stupid cow town who know about it. One is Dent and the other is Fingers, and I'm not even sure about Fingers to tell you the truth. And Fingers, as crazy as he is, isn't crazy enough to do this, especially in broad daylight."

"True but Dent isn't either."

Wilde blew smoke.

"Yeah, well, it wasn't the boxer. He was with me

the whole time."

"Maybe they weren't after the money."

Wilde shook his head.

"That's all I have worth taking."

"That's not true. You have me."

He tapped ashes out the window and said, "'Bama, you need to take your foot off the gas for five seconds."

"Why? Are you afraid of the speed?"

"No, I'm afraid of the crash."

"Come on, Bryson," she said. "You've seen me naked. You know what you're missing. You know you can't hold out forever."

He slumped in a chair. Every muscle in his body ached.

Alabama came behind him and rubbed his shoulders.

"Feel better?"

The answer was, "Yes."

He said, "No."

"Lean forward."

He hesitated; then he complied.

Her touch was whiskey.

Her perfume was sex.

The closeness of her body was life itself.

"Maybe it wasn't Dent," he said. "Maybe there's a fourth person in the mix. Maybe the boxer had an accomplice."

"Yeah, but that waitress from the Down Towner—"

"—Nicole Fountain—"

"—Right, her, she only saw one man."

Wilde relaxed his body.

"That feels good," he said. Thirty seconds later he stiffened, got up and grabbed the Fedora. "Come on, we need to take a ride."

"To where?"

"To where we're going."

"And where is it that we're going?"

"To the place we're headed to."

She punched his arm.

"You know what your problem is Wilde? You never stop being you."

They wound through the rush-hour congestion and headed south where the butterflies and magpies and bees and rattlesnakes were. The plan wasn't complicated; it was to get the dead boxer's car somewhere other than where it was. Right now, as it sat, it was a 3,000-pound exclamation point to the effect that someone left it and never came back—so, look around and maybe you'll find him.

Wilde didn't want the body found, at least not while Fingers was still a trigger itching to be pulled.

In hindsight it was stupid to dump the body in the well; it was justice, yes, but it was dumber-than-dung justice.

The miles clicked off.

When they got to the scene, the boxer's car was exactly as it was before at the side of the road.

The keys were still in the ignition.

"We got lucky," he said.

He must have had an expression on his face because Alabama said, "You're thinking,"

He kicked the dirt.

"I'm wondering if I should get the boxer out of the well and move him to someplace I don't have a connection with."

Alabama wasn't enthused.

"Let him be," she said. "No one will find him for twenty years and when they do they won't know who he is, or care." Wilde chewed on it. "Plus, do we really want to be pulling a body to the road and then driving around with it? Not to mention, where are we going to dump it once we do have it?"

Wilde exhaled.

"All right, we'll let the dog lie. You take his car and follow me."

"Where we going? Further south?"

A hawk circled above on strong silent wings, looking for a tasty little fur-ball or an equally yummy snake.

"We'll bring it back to the city and park it down at the end of Market," he said.

"Are you serious?"

He nodded.

"That way it won't be associated with this road or

the country. We'll leave the keys in the ignition. Someone will steal it within two hours."

That was the plan and that's what they did.

There were no complications.

There were no witnesses, at least none that they
saw.

Twilight was pulling a blanket over the city.

Darkness was coming.

"Now what?" Alabama said.

Wilde assessed his body. It was screaming for re-
lief.

"Now we sleep," he said.

"Together?"

DAY

SIX

August 8
Thursday

17

August 8
Thursday Morning

For everyone who was crazy enough to walk into the joint, Honest Joe had a smile as big as his gut, and didn't skimp on either when Wilde pushed through the doors and headed across the lobby Thursday morning. "I'll be damned," the man said. "The Wildman himself, in the flesh."

Wilde surveyed the interior as he lit a smoke.

Three vehicles were inside, spit-shined to perfection. Lots more were out front between the building and the Colfax asphalt, all with prices written in soap on the windshields. In front of it all was large wooden sign:

> *Honest Joe's Used Cars*
> *Buy Here, Pay Here*

"You got some nice rides here, Joe."

"Always," Joe said. "You looking to make a deal?

I'll treat you good, Wildman; you know that. We'll get you out of that little foreign coffin you drive around in and into something with some meat on it."

"What I'm interested in is an old blue piece of crap, one that you already sold. It's been swinging by my house and my office. It's got a temporary tag in the back. The driver looks like a boxer. He wears a suit and has a fancy gold watch."

"He's following you around?"

"Like my own shadow."

Joe darted his eyes and lowered his voice.

"The damnedest thing happened this morning," he said. "I was buying a newspaper and a ten came out of my wallet and blew away. You haven't seen it by any chance, have you?"

Wilde pulled a ten out of his wallet and dangled it in his fingers.

"It didn't look like this, did it?"

Joe studied it and said, "Yeah, I think that's it."

Wilde handed it to him.

"We were talking about blue crap," he said.

"Right, right," Joe said. "I don't know much about the guy. He came in two days ago and bought Big Blue for cash. You want to see the paperwork?"

"You bet."

There wasn't much, basically a bill of sale and temporary registration for one Richard Hunter; no address, no phone number.

"Richard Hunter?" Wilde said.

"He went by Dick."

"So, Dick Hunter."

"Right."

"Doesn't that name sound just a bit strange to you?"

Joe chewed on it and then smiled. "Are you the dick he's hunting or do you think it's the other kind?"

"I don't think it's the other kind. Where was he from?"

Joe scrunched his face.

"He didn't say and I didn't ask. All he said was that he just got into town and needed wheels."

"He just got into town?"

"Right."

"And this was two days ago, on Tuesday?"

Joe checked the paperwork and tapped a finger. "There it is right there, August 6th. Today's the 8th."

Wilde swallowed.

If that was true then the man wasn't in town last Saturday night when Sudden Dance was murdered. That meant that Wilde killed the wrong man at the well. The idea sent bark and snarl into his gray matter.

He shook it off to worry about it later and lit a cigarette.

"Did he say where he was staying?"

"No but he asked me where a decent hotel was."

"What'd you tell him?"

Joe frowned.

"Did I mention that when that ten blew away a

five went with it?"

At the office Wilde found something he liked very, very much, namely Alabama sitting behind the desk with her legs propped up, surrounded by sea of neatness. Everything was back in its place.

He tossed the Fedora.

It hit the edge of the window and dropped to the floor.

"Did you find anything missing?"

"Good morning to you, too."

"Thanks for straightening up. It feels normal in here again."

"You're welcome. Only one thing was missing that I noticed, the gun from the bottom drawer."

Wilde lit a cigarette.

The gun, his spare, was marginal even on its best day. Whoever took it didn't come here for it. He spotted it and said, Why not?

"Good riddance," he said.

"You carved your name in the handle," Alabama said.

Wilde blew smoke.

That was true.

"I'm getting a picture of someone shot and your gun tossed on his body," she added.

"Let them try."

He pulled the paper out of his wallet—the paper he found in the blue piece of crap, the one with the phone number written on it—and handed it to Alabama. "I found this in the boxer's ashtray. Do me a favor and call it and see who answers. When they do just pretend you dialed wrong."

He paced next to the windows as Alabama dialed.

The phone rang.

> *Who am I talking to?*
> *Angel? Angel who?*
> *Angel, I was looking for Peter. Is he in?*
> *Really? Is this the beauty salon?*
> *Oh, it's a law firm. I'm sorry—*

She hung up.

"It's a law firm?" Wilde said.

"Apparently so."

"What the hell would the boxer be doing with the number of a law firm?" He blew smoke. "Go through the phone book and match the number. I want to know what firm it is."

She did.

Her face wrinkled.

"You're not going to believe it," she said. "It's that firm where Alley London worked, the one in the Daniels & Fisher Tower—Banders & Rock."

Alley London was the dead body from the well.

Wilde paced.

"This doesn't make any sense. It's getting more confusing instead of better."

"Yeah, so just let it go."

Wilde flicked the butt out the window and grabbed

the Fedora.

"Come on," he said. "We're going to pay a visit to the boxer's hotel."

"What for?"

"To find out who the hell he is."

18

August 8
Thursday Morning

The Mountain View Motel, recommended to the boxer by the honest man, Joe, sat on the Colfax drag next to a tire shop and across from a hotdog joint shaped like a giant hotdog. Wilde didn't want to be associated with the boxer any more than necessary so Alabama went in alone and got the man's room number under the pretext she was supposed to meet him an hour ago.

The man had Room 108, on the first floor at the corner. Wilde entered from the back through the one and only window, checked to be sure the door was locked and then found something of interest, namely a suitcase under the bed.

He swung it up and unzipped it.

Under the clothes were three things of interest.

One was a sawed-off shotgun.

One was a six-shooter.

The other was large manila envelope stuffed with bills. Wilde dumped the contents out on the bed. It was all money, a lot of money, except for one other thing, namely a white business card. It was for a lawyer by the name of Lester Trench in El Paso, Texas.

El Paso.

That was a long, long ways away, in fact all the way down to the Rio Grande. Take a short swim when you get there and you're in Mexico.

Wilde stuffed the card in his wallet, put everything back exactly as he found it—including the money—and then got the hell out of there.

Halfway out the window he came back in.

The money, there was no good reason to leave it here.

The boxer wouldn't be back for it.

Wilde's best guess was that the man had been hired to kill him. The money was some or all of his payment. If that was the case, then Wilde had earned it.

He retrieved the envelope and then got the hell out of there, this time for good.

At the MG Alabama handed him a hotdog and said, "Compliments of Bob."

"Who's Bob?"

"The guy from the joint across the street, the manager."

"He's feeding me? For free?"

"No, he's feeding me but I saved it for you."

"Why's he feeding you?"

"Apparently he likes my legs. You could learn from him, Wilde."

He took a bite.

It wasn't half bad.

Alabama tapped him on the shoulder.

"Guess who drove by while you were inside watching TV," she said.

Wilde chewed and swallowed.

"Who?"

"Your little buddy, Nicholas Dent."

Wilde paused in mid-bite.

"Are you sure it was him?"

"It was him all right. He stared right at me. So did his little office girl, whatever her name is. I got to hand it to him. He's really taking care of his cutie-waitress client, making sure you don't kill her and all that."

Wilde wasn't amused.

He handed her the envelope.

"Don't let that blow away."

Then he cranked over the engine and squealed out.

19

August 8
Thursday Morning

Back at the office Wilde paced next to the windows with a smoke in one hand and coffee in the other, keeping one eye on the street and the other on Alabama counting the money. The total was going to be big but he didn't find himself giving a rat's ugly end.

What he cared more about was staying alive; and keeping Alabama that way too, for that matter.

The boxer was a hitman and Wilde was the target.

That was clear.

That was a given.

Why was Wilde a target? That was the question. The obvious answer was because he killed Sudden Dance, at least in someone's mind. Although it fit, it almost fit too well.

"$2,152," Alabama said. "Keep this up and in a

month or two we'll be able to buy the whole city."

"I don't want the whole city." He blew smoke. "That's a lot of money just to kill me, especially if it was only half up front. Someone really wants me dead. Who?"

Alabama cocked her head.

"It's obviously related to Sudden Dance."

"Is it?"

"Sure, what else could it be?"

"I don't know, but maybe something."

"You're not serious."

He shrugged.

"It could have something to do with one of my cases."

"Which one?"

"I don't know."

Alabama chewed on it.

"It doesn't fit," she said. "Have you been messing around with a married woman?"

"You know I don't do that."

"Well then, we're back to Sudden Dance. Someone doesn't like the fact that you killed her." She smiled. "At least we're getting rich in the process."

"We?"

She nodded.

"I'm cutting you in, honey, don't worry. You're starting to be one of my favorite guys."

Wilde flicked the butt out the window.

"In hindsight I should have taken the money in the boxer's wallet."

"How much was there?"

"Enough."

"Enough to make it worthwhile to go back?"

Wilde wrinkled his forehead and shook his head.

"I don't want Blondie connected with that area, not even an ounce worth."

"We can take the boxer's car; the blue crapper."

Wilde set a book of matches on fire. The pungent odor of sulfur pierced the air and gray smoke snaked towards the ceiling.

He lit a smoke from the flames.

"The only thing worse than someone spotting Blondie in the area is seeing me driving around the dead man's car."

"Let's just rent something then," Alabama said. "We'll stop at the well, I'll drop you off and then keep driving. Half an hour later I'll swing back and pick you up."

Wilde took a deep drag.

The money—maybe a grand or more—was worth the time. It translated to three months pay. The issue wasn't the time; it was the risk. If they went they'd have to be damn sure Johnnie Fingers wasn't on their tail; Nicholas Dent too.

"Well?"

"I'm thinking," Wilde said.

"Come on, Wilde," she said. "Where's your sense

of adventure?"

"I don't have that anymore. I replaced it with another kind of sense, the kind called common."

Alabama smiled.

"The money's just sitting there waiting for someone brave enough to come and get it. Stop thinking about it and let's just do it," she said. "Everything will be fine. We can get Honest Joe to let us use one of his cars for a couple of hours." She ran a finger down his chest. "If you want, we can even move the body. You said you didn't like it there anyway."

That was true.

That was the worst place for it in hindsight; poetic at the time, but now stupid beyond stupid.

He nodded.

"Okay, we'll do it."

"Right now?"

"No, tonight."

"See, you can get to the right answer if someone gives you enough time," Alabama said. "I know a place to dump the body."

Out the window Wilde saw something he couldn't believe. He grabbed the Fedora and ran out the door.

"Where you going?"

"I'll be back!"

Then he was gone, bounding down the rickety wooden stairs two at a time and busting into eye-blinding sunlight down at street level.

20

August 8
Thursday Morning

Wilde ran to the right towards his target, a woman, an Indian woman, Sudden Dance to be precise, unless his eyes were playing a mean trick on him. She was thirty steps ahead, walking briskly. Long black hair swung in tune with her movement, alive with a demonic beat.

Wilde picked up the pace.

The gap closed.

"Sudden Dance!"

At the last second the woman turned. It was Sudden Dance. She stared at him for a heartbeat, almost as if in a trance, and then swung a knife at his face with all the speed of a lightning attack.

Her aim was off, not by much but enough for Wilde to jerk back as the swish of air passed close enough to taste. The movement was so intense and so absolute that his body lost control and pummeled to the sidewalk. The wind shot out of his lungs.

Sudden Dance's face contorted.

Then she lunged at him.

Wilde kicked his foot into her stomach, landing solid. When she fell back he wrestled her to her back and pinned her down.

She struggled with every ounce of strength in her body.

Wilde kept her in place until the fight died.

Then he got to his feet and pulled her up.

Several people were stopped, huddled and watching.

"Go on to where you're going," Wilde said. "It's all over here."

The knife was at his feet.

He kicked it to the side, grabbed the woman by the arm and led her up the street. She resisted, pulling back.

"Where are you taking me?"

He gave her a long, hard look.

Then he released her, lit a cigarette and blew smoke to the side, deciding.

Suddenly he didn't care.

He didn't care why she was still alive.

He didn't care why she tried to kill him.

He didn't care why nothing in his life ever went right.

"You know what?" he said. "Just get out of here."

He turned and walked away.

"I'll be back," she warned. "It's not over. It will never be over."

He stopped and turned.

"Stay out of my life," he said. "I don't know what kind of a sick game you're playing but I'm not interested in it."

"You killed Sudden Dance," the woman said. "You're going to pay for that."

The words landed with the force of a tire iron to the side of his head.

You killed Sudden Dance.

He focused harder on the woman.

She looked like Sudden Dance, but maybe not a hundred percent. At first he thought it was just because she wasn't dolled up and was out in the sunlight instead of the smoky dark of the Bokoray. Plus, he wasn't drunk now; he was a man with the charge of adrenalin in his brain. The more he focused on her, however, the more he wasn't sure it was her.

"Who are you?"

"I'm the person who's going to kill you."

She spit on the ground and walked away.

21

August 8
Thursday Morning

Wilde watched the woman as she left. Her attire was simple, her body was curvy and her stride was strong. She stopped long enough to light a cigarette, tossing a match to the sidewalk, and then kept going, never looking back. Wilde pried his eyes off her and headed in the opposite direction. Ten steps later he stopped, wondering if the thoughts that just wedged into his skull were the best or worst he'd ever had.

He didn't care.

He ran back, grabbed the knife off the ground and caught up with the woman, tapping her on the shoulder as he got to her.

She turned.

Her eyes were the sexiest things Wilde had ever seen.

He held the knife out and said, "You forgot this."

She focused on it but didn't reach.

"I didn't kill Sudden Dance," Wilde said.

The woman searched his face, looking for lies or tricks. She must not have found any because she said, "The word is that you did."

"Well, the word's wrong. I'm going to go have a drink. You can join me or not, your choice."

She hesitated, took the knife and searched his eyes.

Wilde said, "I have a theory who might have killed her. We can talk about it."

They ended up in a dark corner of the Ginn Mill with Wilde's personal bottle of whiskey out from behind the bar and on the table, joined by two almost-clean glasses, his filled with ice. He poured alcohol into both, tapped his against hers and said, "To the truth."

He took a hard swallow.

"Given your resemblance to Sudden Dance, I'm going to take a wild guess and say you're her sister."

The woman pulled a photo out of her purse and passed it across the table. It was a black-and-white, aged, depicting two Indian kids leaning against a horse fence, holding rifles. They looked identical except that one was slightly shorter.

"That's me and Sudden Dance," the woman said. "I'm the one on the right, the taller one. I'm eleven there and she's ten."

"So you're not twins."

"Not in date of birth," she said. "We came out the same, though. It'd be more accurate to say we're copies rather than twins."

"Interesting."

"My name's Jori-Rey, by the way."

"Is that Indian?"

She shook her head.

"I don't go by my Indian name anymore. You said you had a theory who killed her."

Wilde shrugged.

"It's just a theory," he said. "I don't have any proof."

"Tell me."

He tapped out two cigarettes, handed one to the woman and stuck a match.

She leaned forward for the fire.

The top two buttons of her blouse were open.

When she came closer a cleavage took shape.

Wilde's eyes played there as he lit her up.

When he brought them back up she was staring into them, reading his thoughts, his nasty little thoughts.

He didn't care.

"Like I said, it's just a theory. I'm not sure I should tell you. I don't want you running off killing someone who might not have actually done anything."

She blew smoke.

"Just tell me."

He leaned back, deciding, and then leaned in, close enough to lower his voice. He told her about the night in question, every stinking detail of it; how he tried to pick up Sudden Dance at the Bokoray, how he came out to find both her and Blondie gone, how Blondie showed up out in the county with a flat, the whole thing.

She asked questions.

He answered them.

He didn't hold back.

He even told her about finding a body in the well, a body that belonged to a lawyer named Alley London.

Finally he told her about searching Sudden Dance's room. "She had a suitcase under the mattress with a lot of money in it, over five G's. I think the money is why she ended up dead. I think she took it from someone and that's who killed her."

Jori-Rey narrowed her eyes.

"Rojo," she said.

"Rojo?"

"Rojo. It was Rojo's money. He's not the one who killed her though."

"Why?"

"Because he loved her."

Wilde wasn't impressed.

"If you're saying they were lovers, and then she ran out on him and took his money in the process,

I'd say that's a pretty good reason for him to kill her."

"Ordinarily yes. Have you ever heard of Rojo?"

He shook his head.

"No."

"He's not exactly what you'd call a nice man." She splashed more whiskey in her glass and added, "You know where Paso del Norte is, right?"

Wilde frowned.

"I'm starting to feel stupid here—"

"Don't," she said. "Paso del Norte is a border town in Mexico, right across the Rio Grande from El Paso. For the most part it's a great place with really great people leading simple, honest lives. But a lot of it's built on a darker element."

"Meaning what?"

"Gambling, whores, bars, drugs, you name it," she said. "Any of it that's worth anything, Rojo's got his hand in it, either directly or through extortion. He's the devil of darkness."

Wilde mashed his cigarette in the ashtray.

"And Sudden Dance was mixed up with him?"

"Yes."

"It doesn't make sense."

"It's a long story but here's the part of it that's important," she said. "Three years ago, while she was with Rojo, she started taking up with a man on the side. They fell in love, saw each other more and more, and then she got pregnant. Her stomach started to grow. She couldn't destroy the baby, not in a million years, and told Rojo it was his. Rojo believed her. He was a happy man."

"Okay."

"When the baby came out it was half white. Rojo went into a rage the likes of which this earth has never seen. He found out who the man was and killed him with his bare fists right in front of Sudden Dance's eyes. He didn't kill Sudden Dance, though. He didn't let her go, either; he would never let her go, that was the rule from day one. He forced her to stay with him, no doubt at that point hoping she'd fall back in love with him but if she wouldn't then the hell with it, at least no one else would ever have her. He hated the baby with every fiber of his body. When it was four months old, Sudden Dance came back to the Villa one afternoon to find it gone. Rojo said he'd made arrangements for it to grow up someplace else."

She took a swallow of the liquor and leaned in.

"Here's the important part. He made it very, very clear that if she ever left him, he'd have the baby killed; it didn't matter if it happened in six months or six years. If Sudden Dance ever left him, the child would die."

Wilde pictured the murder.

"Was it a boy or girl?"

"A girl, Maria. She's two years old at this point."

Wilde shifted his frame.

"So what was Sudden Dance doing way up here in Denver?"

"Picking up money."

"For Rojo?"

"Right."

"From who?"

"I don't know."

"I'm surprised he let her leave town."

"He had to."

"Why?"

"Because if he kept her reigned in too tight she'd kill herself," she said. "So he let her work as a mule on occasion. It was her indiscretion and he gave it to her."

"Wasn't he afraid she'd cheat on him like before?"

"I'm sure he was," she said. "In a way I wouldn't be surprised if that's why he let her leave. If she had to do it he'd rather not know about it. He'd rather it happen someplace else where he wouldn't get embarrassed by the rumors and be forced to act. He knew she'd come back. She had to, otherwise Maria would be killed."

Wilde lit two more smokes and handed one to Jori-Rey.

"Do you really think he'd kill a kid?"

"You're joking, right? That's part of how extortion works. You threaten to kill loved ones; and you set examples so there's no confusion."

22

August 8
Thursday Afternoon

The bar was dark, the whiskey was strong and Jori-Rey was every damn bit as intoxicating as Sudden Dance. Wilde found his thoughts turning nasty. Images popped into his head, rude images of driving the woman back to his place and taking her deep and hard and all-consuming and not stopping until he'd turned her into a sweaty, lust-soaked animal with nothing left of her existence except the fire in her veins and the thrashing of her body.

"Wilde, you there?"

The image snapped off with all the subtleness of an 8mm tape splitting in two and slapping over and over as the reel spun.

He tapped ashes into the tray.

"I need you to do me a favor," he said. "There's

a detective in town by the name of Johnnie Fingers. He's convinced himself that I killed Sudden Dance. He's going to take me down as hard as he can."

"If you didn't kill her you don't have anything to worry about."

Wilde cocked his head.

"That's not the way it works," he said. "Fingers will make stuff up if he has to. It's all in the name of justice because he knows in his heart I'm the killer. What I need you to do is go down to Fingers' office with me and pretend you're Sudden Dance. We'll show him you're still alive. That will put an end to it."

Jori-Rey leaned back.

"No."

"No?"

"No, I can't," she said. "I'd like to but I can't."

"I don't get it—"

"Play it out," she said. "We trick Fingers into thinking that Sudden Dance never really got killed. What happens next is that word to that effect will get out on the street and then it will eventually make its way to Rojo. Now, when Sudden Dance doesn't return to him—which she won't because she's dead and I can't pretend to be her—he'll have only once conclusion to reach, namely that she left him. As soon as that fire enters his brain he'll kill Maria. Do you understand what I'm saying?"

He did.

He did indeed.

"In fact, even being here with you in public is dangerous," she said. "I'm sorry Wilde. You seem like a nice guy but I can't put Maria's life on the line, I just can't."

"No, that's okay, I get it. I'd do the same thing. Don't feel bad about it."

She leaned in and put her hand on his.

"You're a private investigator," she said. "Maybe you can figure out where Maria is. If we can get her to a safe place, then we'll be in a position to go to Fingers like you want."

Wilde tapped two new smokes out of a pack, lit them from the hot end of his and handed one to Jori-Rey, who dangled it between her lips.

"Do you have any idea where she is?"

"Maria? No. In fact, I've spent every penny I could get my hands on hiring people to find her. No one's even gotten close. The last guy I hired, a PI named Cisco Bandaras out of Los Angeles, had a theory that the only way to find her was to get close to the one person who knew where she was, namely Rojo himself—or someone he may have told, which would be someone close to him. He went down to Paso del Norte to snoop around. He knew the town and had some connections there. He knew the language and the haunts and the ways. He could blend in better than the most invisible ghost."

She paused.

"And?"

"And he never came back."

Wilde pictured a knife slicing through a throat.

He could hear the gurgling of blood and the monotone thump of the man's body dropping to the floor.

"Look," he said. "Sudden Dance died because of that money. It belongs more to you than me. It's a little over five Gs. I'm going to give it to you. Just be careful it doesn't get you killed."

Jori-Rey shook her head.

"I don't want it."

"Why not?"

"It's cursed," she said. "If you want to give me something that I really want, give me Maria. Find her so I can take her someplace safe and raise her. I'm the only blood she has left."

Wilde took a long drag on the smoke and felt his world shift.

Everything was suddenly different.

He'd help the woman.

He'd help her all the way to the ends of the earth if need be.

23

August 8
Thursday Night

Thursday night after dark an evil storm rolled out of the Rockies and attacked Denver with everything it had. Wilde punched through it from behind the wheel of an oversized '49 Studebaker, heading south out of the city with the headlights barely able to cut through the weather to define the road.

Alabama rode shotgun.

Between the two of them on the bench was Jori-Rey. Bringing her might be a mistake but it was too late to worry about it now. Her thigh pressed against Wilde's.

Jori-Rey had a theory about the boxer, namely that Rojo had gotten the word on the street that Wilde killed Sudden Dance. He hired the boxer first and foremost to kill Wilde and secondly to recover the money that Sudden Dance had picked up from whoever it was she picked it up from.

Wilde agreed.

It fit perfectly.

"The boxer won't be the last," Jori-Rey said. "He'll just be the first. If I were you I'd turn myself into a ghost and disappear. Denver will never work for you at this point, not unless you want to spend the rest of your life looking over your shoulder. Go somewhere else, get a new name—I picture you as a Slade, maybe Paul Slade or something like that. Start fresh."

Wilde made a face.

"That's not my style."

"Yeah, well, make it your style. Lose the macho stuff because if you don't it will kill you."

"Then I die," Wilde said. "Can you light me a smoke?"

Thirty minutes later they reached the well. Alabama took the wheel and drove off into the storm. The taillights disappeared almost immediately. Wilde and Jori-Rey cut into the brush armed with a flashlight that could have had stronger batteries. Over Wilde's left shoulder draped a 100-foot coil of rope.

The ground was saturated.

The storm was fierce.

They were barely off the road when something strange happened.

Headlights came out of nowhere, going the same

direction as Alabama, a couple of minutes or so behind. They turned into taillights as they swept past
and then vanished.

They were going fast.

It could just be a rough coincidence.

Wilde's gut, however, told him otherwise.

"That's not good," he said.

"So what do we do?"

He searched for options, found none and said, "I
put my gun in the glove box. Alabama saw me do it."

The well appeared exactly where it should.

Wilde shined the flashlight down to be sure the
boxer's body was still there.

It was.

He tied off the rope to the trunk of a scraggly
pinion pine and climbed down.

The body stank.

He got the man's wallet out his pocket and stuck
it in his own. He tied the rope around the man's chest
and climbed back out. Then he pulled the body up
and got it over the edge of the well onto the ground.

He shined the light into the man's face and let
Jori-Rey take a good look.

"Do you know him?"

"No."

Wilde wiped water out of his eyes and contemplated the best way to get the body back to the
road. He didn't want to touch it more than he had to

and considered dragging it with the rope. On closer thought, that would leave a trail, not to mention that the body would probably snag every ten feet. He picked the man up in his arms like a baby, but the weight was too much. He dropped it down, got his strength and then flung the body over his shoulder with one solid motion.

That was better.

That was doable.

"Lead the way."

It took an effort, an insane effort, but they eventually got to the road where Wilde dropped the body just out of sight.

The storm pummeled down.

The world was black.

Wilde stared down the road in the direction Alabama would come from.

No headlights appeared.

A minute passed, then another and another.

Nothing changed.

Everything remained black.

The world remained empty.

Jori-Rey wrapped her arms around Wilde and said, "She'll be here any minute. Don't worry."

24

August 8
Thursday Night

Time passed and Alabama still didn't show up. The storm was under Wilde's skin. The possibility of being abandoned out in the middle of nowhere with a dead body wasn't helping matters.

Forty-five minutes had passed.

Alabama was supposed to swing back in thirty. She'd have trouble finding the exact drop-off point so she was supposed to flash the lights when she got in the area. That way Wilde would know it was her and he'd flag her down with the flashlight.

Suddenly something happened.

Headlights came up the road at a high speed. They were flashing. A second car followed, dangerously close. Bursts of orange came from outside the passenger window.

"They're firing at her!"

Wilde saw that.

He said nothing.

He needed action and needed it now.

He had no gun.

He had no knife.

The second car rammed Alabama's bumper. Her headlights jerked with the motion and she fought to keep control.

Wilde swept the light to the ground and didn't let up until he found a rock. It was the size of a baseball, heavy in his grasp. As Alabama approached Wilde pointed the flashlight at her at the last second.

Then he hurled the rock at the second car with every ounce of strength his arm could muster.

The windshield exploded.

The vehicle jerked to the right, tried to counter and pitched into a death roll, eventually grinding to a stop on the roof.

"Stay here!"

Wilde ran towards the vehicle with one thought and one thought only, namely to pound the men into oblivion if they were conscious, before they could re-gain their senses and get their deadly little weapons back in hand.

The driver was dead, grotesquely dead.

His face was a bloody pulp.

His neck was broken, leaving his head to hang with a bizarre twist. Wilde wrestled the man's wallet out of his pocket and shoved it in his own, not for the money if there was any, but to know who he was.

The other man wasn't in the vehicle.

He must have been ejected.

Wilde swung the light to the ground and swept it back and forth, searching, knowing he was a sitting duck because of the light but counting on the violence of the roll to rip the gun out of the shooter's hand.

The man didn't appear.

Wilde searched more, quicker, with more intensity.

Still the man didn't appear.

Alabama returned, shaken to the core but beautifully alive, and getting a tight full-body squeeze from Wilde to prove it. The back window was shattered and there were bullet holes in the dash but she was unharmed.

"There were two men in the car, right?"

"Yes."

"Then one got away."

"Forget him. Let's just get out of here."

Wilde contemplated leaving the boxer there for the police to find, as some unknown piece of a mysterious puzzle. Then he thought better of it; the body was too decayed to be part of the accident. So they put it in the Studebaker's trunk, drove into the mountains and dropped it over a high jagged cliff. The bears and coyotes and hawks would find it long before a human did. Twenty-four hours from now it would be unrecognizable. The important thing was that it wasn't at the well any longer, the well that Fingers had Wilde connected to.

Ironically, the new accident was at the well.

The murder attempt wasn't against Alabama, that's what Wilde told her once and then twice and then two more times. "They were trying to get me. They thought I was in the car. They didn't know you dropped me off. So don't worry, no one's out to get you."

"Okay."

"Plus tonight's safe in any event. If the missing guy is actually still alive it probably isn't by much, not to mention he's stuck out in a storm in the middle of nowhere."

Out of an abundance of caution, though, he didn't want her to be where anyone could find her tonight, so he got her a room at the Kenmark and tipped the receptionist a soggy five to make sure that if anyone came in looking for her they didn't find her, not in a hundred years.

Wilde wrote down his phone number and said, "If anyone asks about her, give him the big stone face and then call me at home."

"You bet."

Then he headed home through the storm with Jori-Rey still in the car.

He checked the house, found no unwanted scumbags lurking in the corners, and brought Jori-Rey in. They were no longer dripping but were clammy clingy damp. Wilde got a hot shower going for her, laid a dry T-shirt, fresh boxers and pair of pants out on the bed, and closed the door.

With a beer in hand, he plopped down on the couch and went through the driver's wallet.

Inside was money, over a G in twenties.

It brought a smile to his face.

Being a target was starting to have its advantages.

Also inside was a condom and more interestingly a folded page torn out of the yellow pages. It was the listing for investigators, meaning Wilde's number and office address.

Outside the storm raged.

The windows rattled.

Lightning flashed and thunder rolled over Denver with the force of a thousand maniac drums.

The shower shut off.

Two minutes later Jori-Rey walked into the room wearing the T-shirt but not the pants. Her legs were strong and shapely, capable of rivaling Norma Jean's six out of seven days. Her hair was wet and incredibly erotic. Her eyes had a depth that Wilde had never seen before.

She turned off the lights.

Then she came to the couch, straddled Wilde's lap and brought her lips to his.

DAY

SEVEN

August 9
Friday

25

August 9
Friday Morning

Friday morning a well-dressed man walked into Wilde's office. He was strong, intense and polished; the kind of ego-infested guy who could hold his own in an alley fight during the day and chat-up the high-society dollfaces at night. An expensive suitcase dangled from his left hand. He sized Wilde up and said, "My name's Jack Strike. I'm a lawyer with a law firm here in Denver by the name of Banders & Rock. I'd like to retain your services for a project if you're available."

Banders & Rock.

Banders & Rock.

At first Wilde couldn't place why the name was familiar. Then he remembered. Banders & Rock was the law firm where Alley London worked, the woman Wilde found in the well.

Wilde tapped two cigarettes from a pack and offered one to Strike, who declined. Wilde lit his and said, "I'm a little surprised you're here."

"Why?"

"I thought all your work went to Nicholas Dent."

"It does, normally, but this is something that needs to be done right away and he's tied up." He pulled an envelope out of his jacket and set it on the desk. "That's $1,500, half-payment upfront. You get another $1,500 when the job's done."

Wilde focused on the envelope but didn't pick it up.

"That's a lot of money," he said.

"We buy confidentiality in addition to services," Strike said. "I assume your services come with confidentiality—"

Wilde nodded.

"A hundred percent worth. So what's the job?"

The man set the briefcase on the desk and said, "The job is to deliver this to a lawyer in El Paso."

"El Paso, as in Texas?"

"Right."

"Just deliver it? Nothing else?"

"No, nothing else. You drive down, you hand it over, you drive back and get your other $1,500. If everything goes without a wrinkle, you'll see more work from us down the road."

Wilde focused on the briefcase.

Then he raised his eyes and stared into Strike's.

"So what's inside?"

Strike frowned and shook his head.

"You don't need to know that," he said. "It's for your own good, to help you keep the confidentiality part of your commitment. The briefcase is locked. Here's the important part; it's to stay that way at all times. You're not to open it and you won't have the key. If you pry it open or force it open in any way, it will show and we'll know that you did it. See the hinges and hardware and leather? They're all pristine, without a scratch or a mark. Your job is to make sure they stay that way, meaning that they're not tampered with. I'll repeat it again just to be absolutely sure we're on the same page. You are not to open the briefcase or attempt to open it under any circumstances. You're to deliver it and that's all. Is that something you can do?"

Wilde blew smoke.

"How do I know there's not something illegal in there?"

"You know it because I'm telling you that right here and now," Strike said.

Wilde wrinkled his face.

"That's a lot of money to be a delivery boy."

"It's fair pay."

"It seems a little more than fair to me."

Strike shifted his body.

"There's a little twist I haven't mentioned yet. There may be people who will try to take it from you.

Be sure they don't."

"Who?"

"Unknown."

"But someone?"

"Possibly. To be honest, that's why you're getting the case instead of Dent. Between you and me,
Dent's a good sneak but he's not much of a man."

Wilde focused on the briefcase.

"Who do I deliver it to?"

"A man named Lester Trench."

Lester Trench.

Wilde knew the name.

The man's business card was stuffed in the envelope of money Wilde found in the boxer's hotel
room.

His heart raced.

Something was going on, something dangerous.

He needed time to figure it out.

It was too complicated to piece together in the
next two minutes.

"If you want the job, I need you to leave right
away," Strike said.

"You mean today?"

"No, I mean right now, as soon as I leave."

Wilde chewed on it.

He couldn't let the case get away.

It had secrets to tell him.

He blew smoke and said, "I'll need an hour to
wrap a few things up."

Strike looked at his watch.

"Okay. Be sure you take your gun."

26

August 9
Friday Morning

At the window Wilde set a book of matches on fire and watched the lawyer, Jack Strike, through the flames as the man slid into the passenger side of a shiny black Lincoln that pulled off as soon as the door shut. When the vehicle turned at the corner Wilde got a good enough look at the driver to tell it was a female. A fashionable hat kept her face from view.

She was probably Strike's personal secretary, that or a lawyer in the firm, or possibly a client.

It didn't matter.

Two minutes later Jori-Rey showed up, her face obscured by oversized sunglasses and an equally offensive hat. In her hand was a bag of donuts. She set it on the desk, pulled one out—cake with chocolate frosting—and held it to Wilde's mouth.

He took a bite.

She took the second and said, "You were pretty rough last night."

"Sorry."

"That wasn't a complaint." Her eyes fell to the briefcase. "What's that?"

"That' something I'm going to take to El Paso."

"El Paso?"

He nodded.

"That Rojo's territory," she said.

"I know."

Wilde filled her in on the assignment. "Here's the interesting part. It's going to a lawyer in El Paso by the name of Lester Trench. I know he's connected to the boxer—the guy we dumped over the cliff last night. But the guy who hired me this morning, Jack Strike, doesn't know that I know that. The only reason I know about the connection is because I found the El Paso lawyer's business card in the boxer's hotel room."

"So what do you think is going on?"

He tapped two smokes out and lit them up.

"Hold on," he said. "There's another thing of interest. The woman I found in the bottom of the well, Alley London, worked at the same firm as the lawyer who hired me this morning, Jack Strike. The firm's Banders & Rock. I found their phone number on a piece of paper in the ashtray of the boxer's car. So the two lawyers are both connected to the boxer."

"Do you think Strike killed her?"

Wilde blew smoke.

"It's possible, hell, maybe even probable. He's capable of it. Two seconds of looking into his eyes will tell you that."

She wiped frosting from Wilde's lip with her finger and then sucked it off.

"Don't go to El Paso."

"Why?"

"We both know why."

That was true.

He'd end up dead.

He went to the window and looked down.

The lawyer wasn't there.

No strange faces were lurking around.

Still, a sense of danger drifted up.

"I was going to end up there sooner or later anyway," he said. "It may as well be sooner."

"Then I'm coming with you."

Wilde frowned.

"Around me is the last place you should be."

"I'll be the judge of that," she said. "You only need to know one thing. If you go, you'll either have me sitting in the seat next to you or following behind in my own car. If it ends up being the latter, you won't be able to put your hand on my leg."

Wilde blew smoke.

"This isn't a game."

She hardened her face.

"No, it isn't. I'm going to Rojo. He's either going to tell me where Maria is or I'm going to kill him. I don't care if it takes the rest of my life."

Wilde pulled a donut out and took a bite.

"Does he know about you?"

"You mean that Sudden Dance has a sister?"

"Right."

"No," she said.

"Are you sure?"

"Yes. He was too obsessed with Sudden Dance. She was afraid to tell him there was a second one."

"Why?"

"Because he'd bring her down and fall in love with her too," she said. "That wouldn't end well, not for anyone."

Wilde chewed on it.

"You can ride down, at least part way. I may not bring you all the way in though. Know that from the start. I have to think it through."

"Fair enough. When do we leave?"

He looked at his watch.

"Soon."

Then he handed her three twenties.

"Do me a favor and head over to 16th Street and buy a briefcase as close as you can to this one." He inspected it. "This is a Brownstone. Get the same brand if you can. Be sure it's real leather—tan like this one—and has locks."

"That won't work. When you deliver it the lawyer's key won't fit."

"I'm betting he doesn't have the key," he said. "I doubt Strike would have actually mailed it. I'm banking on the fact that all the lawyer has is a description of what it looks like and a plan to pry it open after he gets it. While you're out, get a few changes of clothes too. Something comfortable. Something you can run in. I'll pick you up at the corner of 16th and Delaware at exactly ten o'clock. When you leave here, go out the back way. Okay?"

"Okay."

27

August 9
Friday Morning

As soon as Jori-Rey left, Wilde pried the briefcase open, not giving a fried monkey's brain that he was breaching a client's confidence because the client was a snaky little snake and Wilde's life depended on knowing what type of snake he was dealing with.

Inside were several things.

Two fat white envelopes, wrapped with rubber bands, were stuffed with money. Wilde counted one, which came to five Gs. The other was of similar bulk, making ten total. He wrapped them back up exactly as he found them.

Also inside were three folders, each stuffed with papers written in Spanish, some typewritten and some longhand. Wilde could do a lot of things but reading Spanish wasn't one of them. They might as well be Martian.

He flipped through, nonetheless.

Tucked in back of the last folder he found a sealed envelope marked Confidential.

He opened in.

Inside were a number of photographs. Several were of him, taken without his knowledge, including one looking out his office window. Others depicted Sudden Dance's hotel room, where Wilde found the suitcase of money tucked under the bed; the well, where he found Alley London's body; the Bokoray; and others, all relating to Sudden Dance's murder.

There were also two typed pieces of paper, written in English.

Wilde lit a smoke.

Then he read the papers.

Just as he finished, Alabama walked in with a bag of donuts, which she tossed on the desk and then hopped up next to.

Her tanned legs dangled.

The top two buttons of her blouse were undone.

Cleavage peeked out at Wilde.

"You got rid of me last night so you could do nasty things to your little Indian friend," she said. "That wasn't nice."

"I wanted you safe."

"Safe would have been with you," she said. "I hope she was worth all the effort."

"That wasn't my plan."

"Sure, of course not. Just answer one question for me and do it honestly."

He pulled a donut out and took a bite.

"What is it?"

"Does she make a lot of noise?"

He shook his head.

"Those aren't the kind of things I talk about."

"Yeah, well I do, if you care to know."

"Do what? Talk about them?"

"No, make a lot of noise."

"Alabama, I need you to focus. We have a problem, a big problem."

"The guy from last night who got away?"

"No, something worse."

He filled her in on the new assignment from the fancy-schmancy lawyer, Jack Strike, and tapped on the briefcase. "What he's having me do is deliver a long report by Nicholas Dent, who's been following me around even more than I knew. Dent makes a pretty compelling case that I murdered Sudden Dance, and London Alley too for that matter."

"Well, you have to admit, the shoe fits."

Wilde set a book of matches on fire.

"Most of Dent's report is pretty straightforward and he reaches a lot of the same conclusions that I would if I was the one looking in from the outside," he said. "There's one thing that bothers me, though.

His report says that the witness, that waitress from the Down Towner—"

"—Nicole Fountain—"

"Right, Nicole Fountain—Dent's report says that she said she saw me stab the woman in the alley. That's different than the notes we found when we broke into his office. There, she told him she saw *someone* who was wearing a suit and a hat and could have been me but she couldn't say for sure that it was."

"So he's embellished it a bit."

Wilde nodded.

"Not a bit, a lot. The question is, why?"

Alabama swung her legs.

Her skirt was high.

"Are you actually going to go all the way to El Paso and deliver this stupid briefcase?"

"Yes."

"Then I'm going with you."

He shook his head.

"Too dangerous," he said. "The more I think about this briefcase, the more I think the lawyer who hired me this morning, Jack Strike, I think he killed Alley London. I don't know why yet but my gut tells me he's the one. Then he hired Dent to embellish the facts to put the blame on me."

Alabama made a face.

"That doesn't make sense," she said. "If he was trying to put the blame on you he wouldn't stuff it in a briefcase where no one would ever see it."

Wilde shrugged.

"There are pieces missing, I'll give you that. I'm going to call a man named Big Bob."

"Big Bob?"

"He's going to watch over you while I'm gone. I don't want you more than ten feet from him at any time. Promise me."

She ran a finger down his nose.

"Did you already suspect that?"

"Suspect what?"

"That I get noisy."

He smiled.

"Actually, yes."

"So you do think about it."

"Big Bob," he said. "Don't leave his side and I mean it."

He made a call.

Fifteen minutes later an undersized man in a loose suit and oversized Fedora opened the door and walked in, two inches shorter than Alabama, a hundred and ten pounds if he had rocks in his pockets.

A gun was slung in a leather sheath near his ribs.

His eyes immediately fell to Alabama's legs.

Then they came up.

"Bob, thanks for coming," Wilde said.

Outside on Larimer a car screeched to a stop.

Three men got out.

One was Johnnie Fingers.

The other two were dressed the same.

Wilde grabbed the briefcase and Fedora in one fell swoop, gave Alabama a quick hard kiss on the lips as he ran for the door, and ducked out the back.

28

August 9
Friday Afternoon

Wilde didn't get out of the city often enough. That little reality smacked him squarely between the eyes and punched into his brain as he maneuvered a topless Blondie farther and farther south into the untamed stretches of Colorado.

The scenery was a drug.

The sky ricocheted to infinity.

The sunshine massaged his face.

Jori-Rey sat next to him, her hair blowing, her sundress hiked up for the tan, her smile so incredibly easy, her every word a song, her every expression something to be memorized and stored away.

Wilde was hooked; no, not hooked, hooked hard and deep, way down in his soul where he hardly ever went.

He suspected it last night when he took her there on the couch as the storm rattled the windows and the lightning ripped the sky and every molecule in the universe fell into place.

Now, out here away from the clutter and the pressure and the buzz, it was even clearer.

She had the looks.

She had the body.

She had the depth.

She had the mystery.

"Wilde, are you okay?"

He snapped back.

"Yeah, sure, light me a cigarette, will you?"

She did, plus one for herself.

"I think I might be starting to figure out what's going on," he said.

Jori-Rey twisted her body in his direction.

"Go on."

"We start with the basic premise that Rojo figures that I killed Sudden Dance," he said. "Where he came up with that, I don't know for sure but my gut tells me that my P. I. buddy, Nicholas Dent, has his fingerprints all over it."

"How?"

Wilde took a deep drag.

"Maybe Dent did a background check on Sudden Dance and found out she was Rojo's woman. Maybe he contacted Rojo and offered to give him information, for a price, of course."

"So Dent ratted you out?"

"Right, but whether it was Dent or someone else, it really doesn't matter," Wilde said. "What matters is that Rojo came to the conclusion that I killed Sudden Dance. So, the first thing he does is send the boxer to Denver to kill me. When that didn't work, he sent the two guys from last night. Now he's tired of sending guys. Now he's luring me down to where he is so that he can kill me with his own two hands and watch my eyes pop out of my head."

"So all this is a ploy just to get you down to his lair—"

"Exactly. When we drop the briefcase off in El Paso with that lawyer Lester Trench, there will be men there waiting for me; maybe even Rojo himself."

"Well then, you can't drop the briefcase off."

"We'll see how to play it," Wilde said. "I'm still trying to figure that part out."

"We should just turn around."

Wilde tapped ashes.

"This is the path to getting Maria back. You want her found, right?"

She put a hand on his knee.

"I do but not at this cost."

"Well, we haven't paid anything yet, unless you count gas money."

Up ahead three coyotes loped through the brush near the side of the road. "That's a hell of a way to make your living," Wilde said. "With your teeth."

"I like coyotes."

"Why?"

"They're good hunters."

"Coyotes?"

"Yes. Watch them sometime. You'll be amazed." She paused and added, "When we get down to El Paso I think we should bypass the lawyer and go straight to Mexico. I'm going to pretend to be Sudden Dance. I'll pretend something happened to my memory, that I got hit in the head or something. That'll be why I can't remember a lot of the stuff I should know."

The words ripped through Wilde's gut.

"No."

"If I'm Sudden Dance and I'm alive, Rojo won't have a reason to kill you."

"No."

"I'll get in close. I'll figure out where Maria is. I'll get him to tell me. I'll harass him until he does."

Wilde's chest tightened so much that his foot slammed on the brake. Blondie skidded to a to a halt and Wilde killed the engine.

He grabbed Jori-Rey's arm and squeezed tight.

"We're not going another foot until you promise to stay out of it and not do anything until and unless I tell you."

"But—"

"No buts," Wilde said.

Jori-Rey hardened her face. Then she broke free, got out of the car, slammed the door, flicked the butt on the road and walked off.

"You're a hundred miles from nowhere," Wilde shouted.

"I've walked farther."

Wilde sucked the last drag out of his smoke and dropped it over the side. Jori-Rey continued into the distance, every step another act of defiance

Wilde didn't follow.

He'd let her cool off.

She was a hundred yards away now.

He lit a cigarette.

The woman kept walking.

She didn't slow, not a bit.

She didn't turn around.

Stubborn little thing.

Two minutes passed, then two more.

She disappeared around a bend in the road.

Wilde shook his head three minutes later, defeated, and turned the key, having no option except to get her back in the car and try to talk some sense into her.

No sound came.

The starter didn't crank.

It didn't make a sound at all.

It mocked him with complete and absolute silence.

Wilde slammed his hand on the dash, then got out and opened the hood. He would have never stopped out here in the middle of nowhere if Jori-Rey hadn't been so crazy.

It was her fault.

Suddenly a car came from behind and passed.

Wilde's head was in the engine compartment when it did.

He didn't even know it was there until it was disappearing up the road.

It was a shiny black coupe.

It was heading for Jori-Rey.

Wilde's gut churned.

The problem was electrical; he knew that. The starter wasn't getting any juice. The connections looked good on the battery. Still, there might be hidden corrosion. He wrestled the tool kit out of the trunk, worked the connectors off and gave them a look. They had a green crust on the inside. He filed them clean, reattached them good and tight and tried the key again.

Nothing happened.

He got out and kicked the wheel.

Come on you piece of crap!

29

August 9
Friday Afternoon

I t took ten minuetes for Wilde to figure out what Blondie's problem was, ten infinitely-long minutes. The cure was to wrench down a loose connection at the starter, but by the time he figured it out and stomped on the gas, Jori-Rey had already been gone forever.

Around the bend, she didn't appear in sight.

Worse, she didn't appear up the road, which was fairly straight with a good half-mile visibility.

Wilde pushed the pedal to the floor.

The magnamoss responded.

A mile clicked off, then two.

Jori-Rey couldn't have walked this far.

Wilde's chest tightened.

The woman had to be in the coupe, that was the only explanation. She wouldn't have hitched a ride.

She'd been making a point by stomping off but she wouldn't have gone so far as to abandon him.

She must have been taken; Wilde could picture it, a beautiful Indian woman appearing up ahead through the windshield, so wonderfully alone out here in the middle of nowhere, a shapely swaying sundress, a tasty little morsel to gobble up and throw away.

Ten minutes, that's how much of a lead the coupe had.

Wilde gripped the wheel with both hands and powered Blondie to the edge of losing control, backing off only when the tires squealed or when the ass end started to swing out, and even then hardly at all.

A mile later the road forked.

Wilde skidded to a fishtailing stop, deciding.

Left, that was the way south, the way to Mexico.

Right, that was the wrong way.

Pick one!

Pick one!

Pick one!

He swung to the right, hoping that Jori-Rey had mentioned El Paso or Mexico, hoping that whoever took her knew Wilde would eventually come after him.

A mile passed, then another.

The terrain was high-altitude prairie, framed with mesas in the distance where thunderheads were building.

Then something happened.

A black sedan was pulled over at the side of the road up ahead. Wilde didn't let up on the gas until he was right on it, where he slammed on the brakes and fish-tailed to a stop.

He got out, gun in hand and shouted, "Jori-Rey!"

No one responded.

No one was in the vehicle.

"Jori-Rey!"

No one answered.

He held his breath and listened, turning his head, pointing his ears in every direction. Then he heard something out in the thick prairie brush, something not natural, more like the low baritone of a voice than a bird or act of nature.

He ran that way.

What he saw he couldn't believe.

Jori-Rey was staked out spread-eagle on the ground, struggling against ropes and trying to make all the noise she could through a gag. Her dress was pulled up but her panties were still on. Her legs and chest and arms were drenched in sweat. Her eyes were wild. Her lips were bloody.

She was alone.

Suddenly Wilde's peripheral vision picked up a movement.

He spun to find three men silently charging.

The closest was right on him.

A knife swung at his face.

Wilde twisted far enough to avoid the steel but so fast and awkward that the movement slapped him to the ground. His spine landed on a rock and a violent jolt shot up his back and into his brain.

The man lunged.

Wilde jerked the barrel up and pulled the trigger.

Bam!

Bam!

The man landed on him, lifted his arm to stab the knife down and then collapsed with a limp thud. Wilde grabbed his arm but there was no strength left in it.

The man didn't move.

He was weight.

Wilde shot his eyes up to get the location of the other two men. Four steps away a man threw a rock at his face with every muscle of his body. It hit the other man in the side of his head, crushing his skull and splattering spray into Wilde's face.

He shot.

Bam!

Bam!

Bam!

Another rock came, landing in the dirt not more than a few inches from Wilde's face. He frantically twisted out from under the body.

When he got to his feet, the other two men were running into the terrain. Their speed was fast. Their bodies were strong.

Wilde pointed the gun at the back of the closest one.

His finger hesitated.

He lowered his aim and shot at the man's legs.

Bam!

The bullet landed to the right, exploding the dirt.

The men kept running.

Six bullets, that how many he'd shot.

None were left.

He had more but there were back in Blondie at the other end of the universe.

He cut Jori-Rey loose and pulled her up.

The other two men, who had disappeared into the thickness of the boulders and brush, were suddenly back in sight fifty yards away, not running but coming directly at them with a purposeful stride.

Jori-Rey kicked the dead man in the face.

Wilde pulled her away and said, "We got to go!"

They ran.

Ten steps later Wilde slowed just enough to turn and see if the men were giving chase.

They were.

30

August 9
Friday Night

Friday night after dark the lights of a town appeared in the far distance up the road, shimmering in and out of focus as the road rose and fell. Every bone and muscle and molecule in Wilde's body was beaten to a pulp from the endless hours behind the wheel. Blondie was running on fumes.

Beer, food, a shower and mattress; it was all fast approaching.

They were deep in the guts of New Mexico.

Jori-Rey was asleep in the passenger seat, her head tilted and rocking with the motion of the road.

The black sedan was a memory at this point but one that Wilde kept close. Luckily, he and Jori-Rey had been able to get back to Blondie in time to reload, which brought the two men to a last-second halt. Wilde shot two of the sedan's tires to oblivion as he squealed away. One guy threw a rock that caught

Blondie in the trunk. Wilde almost went back to give the asshole a little tit for tat, and even slowed down, but then thought better of it.

The sedan's tires could be repaired by now.

He had no idea who the men were.

He had no idea what their relation was to the man who forced Wilde to kill him.

They could seek revenge.

They could be coming after him; no, *them.*

They'd had a good look at Blondie. She was a lot of things but she wasn't the kind of girl who could hide very well.

A mile clicked off.

The town got closer.

Then something happened.

Blondie sputtered, as if momentarily choking on a chicken bone, then came back to normal.

Wilde hardened his eyes.

Don't do it.

They were still a ways out, five miles at least.

His gaze fell to the gas gauge, yet again, for the hundredth time this hour. It was limp, hanging way below the E. It had been down in that territory in the past but never this far.

He patted the dash and took some weight off the pedal.

Come on, just a little more.

Blondie kept rolling.

Every inch was a gift.

They were three miles out now, within walking distance if it came to it.

Another mile clicked off and then another.

Blondie sputtered, re-caught her breath, went a hundred yards and then died a final death. Wilde let her roll in neutral as far as she would go and pulled off the road. At the last second a rattlesnake slithered frantically away from the headlights, bringing its body directly in front of a tire. Wilde jerked the wheel but it was too late. Blondie rolled over it with hardly any reaction.

They were a mile from town.

With the road noise gone, the silence was suddenly absolute.

Jori-Rey brought her head up and said, "Wow, look at all the stars."

Wilde pointed his face up.

There were millions of them, so bright that they actually cast a yellow patina over the terrain even without the help of a moon.

"We're going to have to walk," he said.

Jori-Rey stretched.

"Fine with me. I could use it."

Wilde stepped out, wedged the gun into his belt, grabbed the briefcase from the back seat, said "Watch for snakes," and headed for the lights down the middle of the road with Jori-Rey at his side.

"So what's the plan?"

"The plan is to hope this cow-town is big enough to have a motel," he said.

"No, I mean when we get to El Paso."

"I don't know yet."

"I haven't changed my mind, Wilde," she said.

"Yeah, I know."

She slapped his ass.

"Am I too much for you?"

He slapped her back.

"Yes but I'm getting used to it."

The Scorpion's Tail Motel was one of those L-shaped one-story jobs with pull-in parking in front of the rooms. A sign flicked red bulbs on and off—*cancy, cancy cancy*.

The siding was adobe.

The doors were green paint in the second stage of peeling.

The exposed timbers were dark and weathered.

It was probably in good shape back in the day, maybe even plush. Now it was a bag of fleas, no need to bring your own. Out of ten rooms or so, only one had a vehicle in front.

In the office they found a young Mexican girl, no more than sixteen, reading a magazine and listening to the radio, visibly startled when the door opened and someone walked in.

"Is you dad or mom here?" Wilde said.

"They're in the back, sleeping."

"So you're in charge?"

"Yes."

"What's your name?"

"Vida."

"Vida, that's pretty." Wilde leaned on the counter. "Tell me something, Vida. How'd this place get its name?"

"Why, don't you like it?"

"Actually, I do—Scorpion's Tail. It's not your average motel name, so I was just curious."

She hesitated, deciding, and then said, "We don't usually tell strangers, but the place used to be called the Last Chance Motel, on account of how far it is to the next town. Then one night a couple of years ago, a man got killed by a scorpion while he was sleeping in his room. A week later my dad changed the name."

"Interesting," Wilde said. "What room was he in?"

"The last one, 112."

Wilde pulled a twenty out of his wallet and handed it to her. "That's not for the room," he said. "That's for you."

She held it, hesitant, as if it might bite.

"Why?"

"Because someone might come around tonight or in the morning looking for someone who might look like me and my lady-friend here. If they do, what are you going to say?"

"I'll tell them the truth," she said. "I never seen anyone like that."

Wilde smiled.

"That's what I was hoping. We'll take the scorpion room, 112, if it's available."

Jori-Rey nudged him.

"We will?"

"Yes."

"That's six dollars," Vida said. "Should I take it out of the twenty?"

Wilde gave her a ten.

"No, take it out of this and keep the change."

The girl focused on him.

"Who are you two?"

"We're just a couple of ghosts," Wilde said. "We were never here. I'm going to park my car in the back, out of sight, if that's okay."

"Sure. Good luck to you."

31

August 9
Friday Night

L eaving Jori-Rey alone in the scorpion room
with the briefcase, the gun, a kiss on the lips
and her promise that she wouldn't venture
out, Wilde got a can of gas from the station down
the street and hoofed it back to Blondie.

She'd been ravaged.

All four tires were flat, the cause not visible but
undoubtedly slit.

The hood was open.

Wires were cut.

He tried the starter and got no response.

The trunk had been pried open.

Jori-Rey's suitcase was on the ground. Her clothes
were scattered in all directions.

Who did it?

The black sedan guys?

Teens?

Some lowlife driving by and stopping for an opportunity?

Wilde poured the contents of the can into the gas tank, then put the ragtop up, closed the hood and got the trunk lid down and held in position with a rock.

At least she'd be watertight.

He tried the ignition again, just for grins, and got nothing but absolute silence. The wires would need to be replaced or spliced.

He scooped up Jori-Rey's stuff back into the suitcase, tucked it under his arm and started the walk back to town. A hundred yards into it, headlights came from behind, bouncing as if from a stiff suspension, more like a truck than a car. Wilde's first thought was to stick his thumb out but the less people who saw him the better.

The headlights paused briefly at Blondie and then kept moving.

When they came to Wilde, they drifted to a stop.

The vehicle was a ragged pickup, dented and worn, basically dark, blue maybe, with a white front fender. Something under the body rattled, most likely a U-joint.

The passenger window was down.

A strong arm hung out.

A white T was rolled up at the sleeve with a pack of cigarettes inside.

A weathered face came into view.

It belonged to an Indian, with black braided hair

cascading out from under a black cowboy hat. A patina of whiskey radiated. A scratchy radio played from the dash, something hillbilly.

"If you want a ride go ahead and hop in the back."

Wilde hesitated, said "Thanks," and then put a foot on the rear tire and swung up into the bed.

The vehicle took off.

Wilde's mind raced.

The original plan had been to try to stay alive until the morning and take off at the first blink of dawn. That was history. It was doubtful a town this small and this far from civilization had tires that fit, not to mention the wiring issue.

They could be stuck here for days.

The Scorpion's Tail came up on the right. The light was on in Jori-Rey's room. Everything looked normal. Wilde resisted the urge to pound on the cab and instead let the vehicle continue. Three blocks later it came to a stop in front of a bar.

The door was propped open.

Bodies came into view; both men and women, most wearing cowboy hats.

Even from here the noise was already loud and drunk, befitting a Friday night.

Wilde hopped out but left the suitcase in the bed.

The passenger, already out, was a good size; strong, too, he'd be hard to put down in a fight. The driver was his equal. Wilde shook their hands and said, "Let me buy you guys a drink."

Hillbilly music spilled out of a jukebox.

No one paid any attention to it.

It was just noise, barely audible in all the other noise.

They ended up near the back, leaning against the wall with brown bottles in hands, watching the cowgirls play pool. One walked over to Wilde and said, "You got winners, and that will be me."

Fifteen minutes later Wilde walked out with two beers in his gut, a lost game of pool to his credit, and the keys to the truck in hand. Back at The Scorpion's Tail he told Jori-Rey what happened; how Blondie got trashed, how he bought the Indian's truck and how they were going to arrange to get Blondie towed tomorrow to a place called Honest Ed's Garage & Repair.

"There's an honest guy in every town," he said. "Here it's Ed."

Jori-Rey pulled the window coverings to the side far enough to get a glimpse of the truck.

"Will that thing make it?"

"We're going to find out." He set a book of matches on fire, lit two cigarettes from the flames and handed one to Jori-Rey. "I'm going to take a quick shower then we'll go hunt down some food. After that, I'm going to hunt down you, so be warned."

"Be warned yourself."

He headed for the bathroom, got the spray up to temperature, mashed the butt out on the sink halfway done to save the rest for later, and stepped inside.

Nothing had ever felt so good.

Well, that wasn't true, but close.

When he stepped out ten minutes later, Jori-Rey wasn't there; the briefcase was and the gun was but she wasn't. Wilde opened the door to find the pickup gone.

She must have made a food run.

Half his brain raged fire that she was playing so reckless.

The other half anticipated the food.

He was closing the door when his peripheral vision picked up a motion across the street. He went inside without looking directly at it, turned off the lights and then pulled the curtain to the side.

Across the way was a parked car.

The black silhouettes of two men were inside.

One cupped a cigarette in his hand as if hiding the fire. The glow lit his face every time he took a drag.

Five minutes later headlights lit the window coverings with a strong force and then went black. Jori-Rey stepped out of the truck and headed for the door. In her hand was a brown paper bag. Wilde let her in and as he did the headlights on the vehicle across the way came to life and squealed away.

Jori-Rey saw the look on Wilde's face, checked out the taillights as they disappeared down the street and said, "Company?"

"Maybe."

"Who?"

"It's not the black sedan. The lawyer said someone might try to intercept the briefcase. I thought he was lying as an excuse to give me the assignment, but maybe he wasn't."

Inside the bag were tacos, enchiladas and two cans of RC.

They dug in, with the radio on, and Wilde checking the street every other second.

The mysterious headlights didn't reappear.

Jori-Rey grabbed a towel from the bathroom and put it over the lamp, dimming the room but not killing the light completely.

"What are you doing?"

She didn't answer.

Instead her body broke into a dance, almost as if possessed, incredibly free and erotic. Her arms were up. Her feet were bare. Her lips were open.

"I love this song," she said.

"So I see."

She let the music take her, control her, transfix her, slowly unbuttoning her blouse the while, then slipping it off and tossing it to Wilde.

Then her shorts were gone; then her bra.

She was down to her panties.

Her body was perfect.

Every movement shot a new jolt of electricity into Wilde's blood.

He watched for as long as he could.

Then he went to her, hard, a predator pouncing with attack, lifting her up and drawing her tight, pulling her legs open, pinning her back against the wall and not letting her loose, not an inch, not until every pore of his being had his evil little fill.

DAY

EIGHT

August 10
Saturday

32

August 10
Saturday Morning

Wilde woke to light sneaking in from around the window coverings and bolted up with the realization he'd fallen asleep all the way until dawn and then some, solidly asleep, not with half an eye as he'd vowed. Outside, the vehicle across the way was nowhere in sight. Jori-Rey slept peacefully on her back, her exposed chest rising and falling gently with her breath.

The gun was on the nightstand.

The briefcase was under the bed.

He still couldn't figure out the vehicle across the way last night, which mysteriously disappeared minutes after he spotted it and never returned, not once in the hundred times he pulled the curtain back and checked. Nor was it anywhere in the vicinity when he crept out the back window and hugged the shadows up and down the street looking for it.

Still, it had been there for him, or Jori-Rey, or the briefcase—one of them.

He straddled Jori-Rey's stomach, pinned her arms above her head and brought his face close to hers as she woke up. "I have some news for you," he said.

She focused.

"What is it?"

"I like the way you dance."

Five minutes later he was dumping coins in a pay-phone to call the office and confirm that Alabama wasn't there.

She answered.

Wilde frowned.

"You're not supposed to be there," he said. "You're supposed to be laying low."

"Forget about that," she said. "I'm finding out some interesting things about your dead little law-yer-friend, Alley London."

"Alabama, you're not supposed to be finding out nothing about nobody. You're supposed to be not looking for anything, not finding anything, not doing anything except continuing to be alive in some little corner where nobody knows where you are except you and Big Bob."

"Big Bob's with me," she said.

"He's not supposed to be letting you do anything."

"Yeah, well, I have tits, remember?"

"What does that mean?"

"It means Bob likes to see them and in return I get to do what I want."

"Tell Bob he's fired."

"Bob, you're fired," she said. Then to Wilde, "I don't think Jack Strike killed that lawyer from his office, Alley London."

"Why? What'd you find out?"

"It turns out that Alley was leading a double life. She was also working as an escort."

"And?"

"And Nicholas Dent, as we both know, enjoys the ladies of the night."

"So you're saying Dent killed her?"

"I'm leaning that way. I don't have motive yet but think about it. Assume that for some reason Dent wants to kill her. Then, miraculously, Nicole Fountain shows up from out of nowhere and tells him about how she witnessed a murder. That gives Dent an opportunity to kill London and then place her body at the murder scene, meaning fairly close to where your car was found. That way it will look like whoever killed Sudden Dance killed her as well. He found an opportunity to kill her and pin it on someone else, namely you."

Wilde wasn't impressed.

"Leave Dent alone. Just lay low like I keep telling you to do."

Ten minutes later he was behind the wheel of the pickup with the front end pointed south and Jori-Rey slid over next to him on the seat.

Within a mile the town disappeared.

They were back in the middle of nowhere, heading deeper and deeper into it.

Wilde's gut churned.

They'd make El Paso by the end of the day.

He couldn't put off not having a plan for much longer.

He needed to figure out what to do.

"You're thinking," Jori-Rey said.

"Can you light me a smoke?"

"Sure."

Wilde dragged on it until it was half gone and said, "I don't think you should pretend to be Sudden Dance."

"Wilde, we've been over this—"

"I know but Sudden Dance lived with the guy day in and day out for years and couldn't crack where he stashed the daughter," he said. "The chance of the new Sudden Dance doing better is zero."

She frowned.

He had a point.

"There's something else," Wilde said. "I keep picturing you in bed with him. I don't like what I see."

"I'm not going to let him touch me if that's what you're talking about."

"How will you stop it?"

"I'll figure something out. Don't worry about it. Just be around, be my backup." She paused and added, "You're going to need to blend in. We got to get you out of that suit. Are you going to meet with that lawyer in El Paso?"

He blew smoke.

"It's a catch-22," he said. "If I do, I should be able to get some information out of him. He'll see my face though. That's the rub."

"I've been thinking about it," she said. "We'll get some photos of someone else and put them in the briefcase. Then we'll have it dropped off by a cabbie or something like that. Then we'll head across the river and see what happens."

"I still don't like it."

"Have you got something better?"

"Yeah, anything. How about you hole up at a hotel and I'll handle it?"

"How?"

"I don't know yet, but I will."

She cocked her head.

"You'll never get anywhere," she said. "You might be able to kill Rojo if you get real lucky but that's about it. That won't get me Maria."

Wilde went to argue.

No words came out.

"We'll see."

"We have to get in close to him," she said. "I can do that in the first ten seconds. You couldn't do it in a hundred years."

"Like I said, we'll see."

"There's nothing to see," she said. "The only question at this point is how do we get photos of someone else to put in the briefcase? He'll have to be someone who looks at least something like you. He'll have to be a gringo."

"Cute."

"Get used to it," she said. "That's what you're going to be as soon as we cross the Rio." She squeezed his hand. "I'm a little scared. You'll have my back, right?"

He returned the squeeze.

"I like your front better, but yes."

The miles clicked off.

The scenery unfolded scene after scene, then in a rut with more and more of the same as the horizon line got farther and flatter and every sage got to be the same size and color.

The truck occasionally protested with a stutter or a click but never to the point of shutting itself down. Wilde didn't trust it but had to concede it was actually getting the job done.

Blondie.

With any luck she'd been towed by now and not tricked into rotting at the side of the road.

He couldn't get the image out of his mind, the image of Jori-Rey in bed with some violent, self-absorbed jerk. If the guy forced himself on her, he would view it as merely taking what was his. He wouldn't view it as something worse. For that reason, Wilde couldn't kill him, not for that act alone in any event. He'd want to but he wouldn't be able to justify it.

Or could he?

He narrowed his eyes.

Jori-Rey felt good at his side.

She felt right.

She felt like air in his lungs.

A mile later she tossed a butt out the window and said, "I need to use the facilities."

Wilde drifted to a stop but left the engine running.

Jori-Rey headed for a bush.

"Be right back," she said.

"Watch for snakes."

A light breeze slithered through the air.

A hawk floated on a thermal.

The land was flat.

The horizon was far.

The sun beat down with the force of a thousand maniac matches.

Wilde wiped sweat off his brow with the back of his hand.

Something caught his eye, a distant movement. A vehicle was coming from behind, a long ways off, five miles or more, nothing more than a dot at this point but heading this way.

His chest tightened.

"Hurry up," he shouted.

33

August 10
Saturday Night

It was after dark when they came up on El Paso. Two miles out of town Jori-Rey said, "Pull over for a minute, will you?"

"Why?"

"Because I'm scared. I'm not sure I like our plan anymore."

Wilde drifted to the side of the road and killed the engine. Jori-Rey pulled him to the center of the bench, pulled her skirt up and straddled his lap. Her face was close. Her chest pressed against his.

"I'm sorry, Wilde."

"About what?"

"I can't do it," she said. "I can't save you. I'm too scared. I'm afraid Rojo will kill me. I know that's the best way to get him off your back—to make him think Sudden Dance is still alive—but I don't think I can go through with it."

"Good."

"You're not disappointed?"

"I never wanted you to do it in the first place," he said.

"Maybe I'll be able to do it tomorrow," she said. "Right now though, just the thought terrifies me."

"No, not tomorrow. Not ever."

They made love; slow, rocking love.

Nothing had ever felt better.

Nothing ever would.

The new plan emerged quickly. They decided to bypass the El Paso lawyer Lester Trench, at least for now, and head straight into Paso del Norte, which was the continuation of El Paso except on the Mexican side of the Rio.

El Paso was tame, comparatively speaking.

Paso del Norte was the Yin to that Yang, replete with lowly pleasures manifested in bars, music, brothels, casinos, sin and the occasional sound of a fist landing on a face; a magnet for Americans who needed to escape from their brown bag lives, if even for just a few hours or days or weeks.

Crossing the border was easy.

It was nothing more than getting waved through.

Come on in.

Screw our women.

Drink our Tequila.

Give us your money.

Jori-Rey wore sunglasses and kept her head down. No one gave her a second glance.

They checked into a hotel at the end of the strip, a rat-under-the-bed place called El Bonita, with Wilde registering solo and signing no register because there wasn't one, and then sneaking Jori-Rey in the back way.

He hunted down food and whiskey, brought it back and paced as he ate.

"So what's Rojo look like? Do you know?"

The woman fumbled through her purse and pulled out a photo.

"Jori-Rey mailed this to me. It's two years old."

Wilde studied it.

He didn't like what he saw.

The man had a rough, attractive face, framed in thick black hair that fell to his shoulders. His shirt was open, displaying a carved taut chest designed for Friday night fights. It was filled with tattoos, the most prominent of which was a woman straddling a snake. The head coiled up next to hers, looking out, with fangs glaring. The woman's face was familiar.

"Is that Sudden Dance?"

"Yes."

"And the snake I assume is supposed to be him?"

"Yes. He's protecting her."

"From what?"

"I don't know. You, I guess."

Wilde changed into the clothes they picked up earlier; dungarees, black boots and a black T-shirt with the sleeves rolled up. He roughed his hair up and let it flop down. Then he set a book of matches on fire, lit two cigarettes, handed one to Jori-Rey, and rolled the pack into his right sleeve.

"You stay here. Do not under any circumstances venture out."

He didn't have to say why.

Someone might think she was Sudden Dance. The word could spread to Rojo.

She gave him a kiss.

"You look nice. Don't go breaking any hearts."

"Never."

"If I'm sleeping when you come back, wake me."

"Okay."

"Promise."

"I promise."

"Promise me again."

He downed what was left in his whiskey glass and squeezed her long and tight.

"Don't worry, I'll wake you."

"Don't forget."

Then he was gone.

34

August 10
Saturday Night

Dens of decadence lined the strip, loud, pulsing and crowded, hollering with drunken abandon and drumming the warm, muggy night with an edgy beat. Signs flashed; Casino, Bar, Rooms-For-Rent, Live Band, Pool Tables, Happy Hour. Bodies roamed, packing the streets. Painted women hunted prey, strutting their honey and working their come-ons; Wilde waved them off, one after another.

Most said, "Three dollar."

One dark haired beauty in a short red dress gave him a long look up and down, felt his bicep, put her arms around his neck, laid a lipstick kiss on his lips and said, "Free for you."

"Another time."

"How about now?"

"I have to meet a man about a horse."

"Forget the horse. There are more fun things to ride."

He smiled.

"Next time."

It was Saturday night.

The game was on.

The devil was here.

So was Rojo.

Wilde wandered in and out of joints. Lots of men looked like Rojo but weren't, not when he got close and gave them a good peripheral look. He didn't give up. He kept hunting. What he would do when he found the man, he wasn't sure. The first step was to find him, to get a good look at him and figure out what he was up against.

He was on the street contemplating his next move when arms wrapped around his stomach from behind. He turned to find the red dress.

"Still free," she said.

He studied her.

Then he grabbed her hand and said, "Let me buy you a drink."

"Sure."

"Have you ever heard of a man named Rojo?"

"Yeah. I don't like him."

"Where does he drink?"

Her eyes flicked up the street and landed on a flashing green sign, El Dog Tequila.

"Up that way."

Wilde pulled a ten out of his wallet and handed it to her. "I don't want you to lose money while you're with me. Is this good for an hour or two?"

She studied it.

"You don't want sex?"

"No, just hang on my arm."

She stuffed the bill in her bra and rubbed her stomach on his.

"My name is Rio."

"Joe," Wilde said.

El Dog Tequila was a dog all right, a loud, packed, wild, drunken dog. The women were wanton, the men were rough and the light was dark. A band on a low stage at the far end cranked out inebriated notes and sang in Mexican. They weren't bad except for the drummer, who was an affront to every beat known to man.

Wilde pushed to the bar with Rio behind, her hand on his belt to keep from getting separated.

He kept a peripheral eye out for Rojo but didn't scout the room.

He didn't want to look like he was looking for someone.

Rio rubbed her chest on him and hung close.

She smelled nice.

A brown bottle in Wilde's hand and a double shot of Tequila in Rio's, they pushed through the crowd towards the band, where the cause of the problem became apparent. The drummer was drunk, sloppy drunk, barely able to stay on the throne. Halfway through the song the inevitable happened.

He fell off.

The rest of the band played for a few bars, waiting for him to get up.

It didn't happen.

The music stopped.

The singer poured beer on the man's face and got a reaction, but not much, not enough to even make the guy open his eyes. He curled into a ball; that was it.

Wilde had a crazy thought, told himself not to do it but couldn't stop. He handed the beer to Rio, headed over and picked the drumsticks off the floor, then took a position at the kit.

He lit a cigarette, took a deep drag and dangled it from his lips. He twirled the sticks and said, "Let's go."

They stared at him.

Then the singer howled and turned to the crowd.

Wilde beat the sticks together four times and then the music exploded on the one beat. He didn't know the song but figured the pattern out good enough to lay in the fills at the right time and to change from the hi-hats to the ride where he should. At the end the bass player gave him a cue and they all ended together, remarkably clean.

The crowd howled.

Rio came over, planted a sloppy kiss on his face and handed him a fresh beer. He took a long swallow, set it on the floor and looked at the bass player. The man nodded his head four times indicating the tempo, which was slightly faster than the last song.

Wilde beat the sticks.

The music took off.

Five songs later Wilde spotted what he came here to spot, Rojo, cutting through the crowd and casting an inquisitive eye at Wilde—a gringo he'd never seen before, playing with the house band. Their eyes locked, just for a fraction of a second, and then broke away as if two tornados colliding.

The man was bigger than Wilde, six-three or four, and meatier too.

His arms were pythons.

His face was strong and manly.

Two women flanked him, beautiful women, nicely dressed, moving with him as one.

Three men followed behind.

They looked like killers on a leash.

Wilde stayed with the band until the dog closed, not wanting to leave them dry and high. Then he walked a seriously intoxicated Rio to her place—a cheap, one-room flat—got her tucked in, planted a kiss on her cheek, left a second ten on kitchen counter, and headed for home, The Bonita.

If I'm sleeping when you come back, wake me.

Okay.

Promise.

I promise.

Promise me again.

When Wilde got to the hotel, something was wrong. The door wasn't closed all the way; almost but not quite. It wasn't latched.

He pushed it in with his foot.

The lights were off. The on-now, off-now, blinking of the hotel sign brought the room in and out of a soft blue focus.

Everything looked normal.

He stepped in and closed the door.

"Jori-Rey."

No one answered.

Then an eerie rattling sound came from the bed.

He flicked on the lights.

What he saw jolted every fiber of his body.

35

August 10
Saturday Night

On the bed was a rattlesnake tethered to a hatchet. A thin leather cord was wrapped around the snake's body several times and then tied off. The other end was fixed to the hatchet, with three or four feet of separation.

Jori-Rey wasn't in the bed, under it, in the closet or in the bathroom.

She was utterly and absolutely gone.

The briefcase was gone.

So was the gun.

Wilde approached the bed.

The snake was coiled, bobbing its head in a death trance and shaking its tail to a demonic beat. Its cold lifeless eyes stared into Wilde's soul with an evil intent.

Blood was on the pillow, not a lot but enough to

jack an image into Wilde's brain, an image of Jori-Rey fast asleep and then waking when someone entered the room, at first thinking it was Wilde, then realizing it was a stranger with hurt in his eyes. Before she could even sit up the blow came, it came hard, it came with a force that made colors explode in her head before it sucked her into darkness.

Rojo!

This was his sick little work.

Wilde's chest pounded.

What to do?

What to do?

What to do?

He couldn't concentrate, not with the viper the way it was. He pinned the snake's head under a pillow and kept it immobile while he untied the cord from the body. Then he sandwiched it in the pillow, carried it out behind the hotel far enough into the wild to where it wouldn't be a bother and let it go.

Then he headed to Rio's in the truck, with the hatchet on the seat next to him and a smoke wedged overly tight in his mouth.

The woman was asleep and not wanting to respond to the pounding, not until it got too loud and too long to ignore. She opened the door, saw it was Wilde and put him in a tight hug.

Wilde pulled her inside and closed the door.

He showed her the hatchet and said, "This was in

my hotel room when I got back, tied to a rattlesnake."

The woman's face etched with fear.

"Rojo," she said. "He's a hatchet man. That's his favorite way to kill people. He's been doing it since he was fourteen; at least that's the rumor. He does it slow. He chops off this and chops off that. It's sick, sick stuff."

Wilde exhaled.

"Where does he live?"

The woman shook her head.

"No," she said.

"What do you mean, no?"

"No, forget about him. What you need to do is get out of town and you need to do it right now, otherwise you're dead and not in a pretty way," she said. "I'll help you."

Wilde hardened his face.

"He took a friend of mine."

"Who?"

"A woman," he said. "Where does he live, do you know?"

"No."

"Do you know anyone who does?"

"No, not tonight."

Wilde twisted the hatchet in his hand and slumped on the couch. The weight of the day was suddenly on him, the endless driving, the drumming, the eyes constantly open, not closing for even a brief rest, not once in over twenty hours.

The exhaustion was palpable.

Rio rubbed his shoulders.

"You're a mess. Come to bed."

DAY

NINE

August 11
Sunday

36

August 11
Sunday Morning

Wilde woke Sunday morning with a bad, bad, really bad feeling in his gut. Jori-Rey was gone. Wilde would die later today, or if not today soon, chopped to death one piece at a time by a madman with a hatchet. It wouldn't even be important. It would be a ripple from a pebble, hardly noticeable to anyone in the universe, at least this part of it.

Destiny was unfolding.

He could squirm against it but in the end it would consume him. He'd never seen it before—not this close; not even in the war—and now that he had he realized just how real it was.

It was 10:30, long past what he wanted.

He got off the couch and checked on Rio.

She was in the bed, naked on top of the covers,

passed out and breathing with a deep, hard rhythm. He showered, got dressed, lit a cigarette and then shook Rio until her mocha body woke up and rolled over.

"Morning," he said.

She focused and then reached for his cigarette and took a long drag, then another before handing it back.

"It's too early."

Wilde kissed her forehead.

"I'm heading out. I wanted to thank you first for letting me stay here last night."

She stretched.

Then she grabbed his hair, pulled his head down and kissed him hard on the lips.

"When will you be back?"

"I won't."

"Don't say that."

"It's better for you if I don't. The middle's not a good place to be, not on this one."

"Screw the middle," she said. "Come back this afternoon. That will give me time to ask around and find out where Rojo lives. That's what you want, isn't it?"

"Yes but don't."

"Too late, I already am. Promise you'll come back."

Promise.

Promise.

He'd made a promise yesterday, a promise to wake

Jori-Rey up when he got back.

"I'll come back but only to make sure you're okay," he said. "In the meantime stay out of it. Don't talk to anybody. Do we have a deal?"

She wrapped her arms around his neck, pulled his chest to hers and whispered in his ear, "Whatever you want. Be careful."

Lester Trench, the El Paso lawyer Wilde was supposed to deliver the briefcase to, wasn't hard to track down. He lived in modest standalone adobe on the outskirts of town a half mile from the river, at the end of a quiet gravel lane that backed to rabbit brush and dead prairie.

He was surprised when Wilde knocked on the door here at home, but only to a point, and turned out to be a skinny man in his mid-thirties with a shifty face. Behind him, in the kitchen, was a small Mexican wife and two half-breed kids.

He said to the woman, "Just a little business," and stepped outside. His eyes fell to the truck. "Someone said you had a little foreign car."

Wilde hardened his face.

"I don't have the briefcase."

"I know."

"Rojo has it."

"I know," the lawyer said. "He called me."

"Just to be clear, the whole briefcase thing was just a way to lure me down here so Rojo could kill me, right?"

Trench spotted the pack of cigarettes rolled up in the sleeve of Wilde's T and said, "Do you mind?"

Wilde tapped two out, lit Trench's and then his own.

"You're a hard man to kill," Trench said. "Rojo got tired of handing the work to someone else and decided to do it himself."

"By luring me down here—"

Trench nodded.

"When you delivered the briefcase to me, I was going to tell you to take it across the border into Paso del Norte for its final delivery."

"Where Rojo would be waiting."

"Yes."

"Just to be clear, you were the man who hired the guys up in Denver to kill me. I found your business card in the first guy's room."

Trench frowned.

"Did I hire them? Technically yes but only as a conduit. I do things for Rojo and he shows his appreciation. If I didn't do them someone else would."

"So you're not doing anything wrong, not in your mind—"

He blew smoke and said, "When Rojo's men showed up at your hotel last night, it was to leave the hatchet there for you."

"Why?"

"It's for you to use later if you were brave enough

to get it off the snake," trench said. "That's not what's important here though. What's important is that when Rojo's men showed up, they didn't know there was a woman in the room. But there was and now we all find out that Sudden Dance is actually alive. In hindsight the fact that you killed her has turned out to not be all that true after all."

The words hit with the force of a brick to the brain.

Somehow Jori-Rey convinced Rojo that she was Sudden Dance.

She was alive but for how long?

"Unfortunately," Trench added, "that doesn't get you off the hook. Rojo is still going to kill you and I'm not talking about in a pretty way."

Wilde took a deep drag.

"Why?"

"Don't play dumb." He shifted his face and added, "You're by her side when you shouldn't be. Let me ask you something. Did you sleep with her?"

"That's none of your concern."

The lawyer wrinkled his face.

A jackrabbit scampered through the brush.

"Personally, I don't care one way or the other. Rojo's going to ask the same question, though. If he sees the same answer on your face that I do, rest assured your death will be so long and painful that you'll want it a hundred times over before he lets you have it. If I were you I'd hop in that big old rust-bucket of yours and run so hard and so fast and so far that even I wouldn't know where I was anymore."

Wilde dropped the butt to the ground and mashed it out with his foot.

"Where does he live?"

"Rojo?"

"Yes, Rojo."

The lawyer chuckled.

"You really don't understand what's going on here, do you?"

37

August 11
Sunday Afternoon

The attorney's office was on the main strip in downtown El Paso, on the second floor of an ornate gray building. A kid of ten or eleven picked at a guitar as he slowly strolled down the street. Wilde parked a block away, hoofed it down the alley behind the buildings and made entry by busting a window from a fire escape at the rear.

No one was inside.

It was Sunday afternoon.

The air was quiet and thick with heat.

Guitar strings chimed thinly, almost too faint to be heard. Wilde looked out the window and found the kid sitting on the stairs of the building next door, a bank.

"I do things for Rojo and he shows his appreciation."

Those were the words that came from Trench's

twisty little lawyer-lips.

Those were the words now driving Wilde.

With any luck, one of the things that the lawyer did for Rojo was place Sudden Dance's child, Maria, after Rojo killed the father. With even more luck, there was a file somewhere in this tomb that indicated where the child went.

It was a long-shot but that's what you took when all the short-shots were in short supply.

The guts of the joint were spacious and broken into several rooms; a reception area, a meeting room with a long wooden table, a small kitchen, a file room, a bathroom and Trench's main office. Expensive furnishings and heavily framed original oils, mostly western landscapes, indicated that a man of presence and taste inhabited the place.

Smoke permeated the air.

Ashtrays were replete, each stuffed with dead soldiers, some marked by red lipstick but most not.

Wilde lit a Camel.

The smoke was magic in his lungs.

The bits of tobacco that wiggled out of the end and stuck on his tongue were like old friends.

He searched the file room, putting everything back exactly as it was, nothing more than a ghost. He found nothing relating to Rojo.

He got the same result from the lawyer's office.

Half an hour and four cigarettes had gone by.

All he had to show for it was a big fat zero-filled

nothing.

There was nowhere else to look. None of the other rooms contained files of any sort, Rojo or otherwise. In hindsight the lawyer was too smart to leave a paper trail. Wilde should have known that from the beginning.

He lit a new butt, slumped down in the leather chair behind the desk and turned his thoughts to his own mortality.

He'd be dead soon.

Surprisingly he was getting used to the idea.

It had to happen sooner or later anyway.

He'd lived a good life.

He'd been more fortunate than most.

He had no right to complain.

Alabama would miss him.

That counted for something.

Suddenly a noise came from the adjacent room. A key twisted in a lock, a doorknob turned, a door sung open and then closed none too gently. Wilde ducked under the desk and mashed the butt out on the wood. Gray smoke circled up and accumulated under the drawer.

It didn't take long to figure out who entered, it was a man and a woman.

It also didn't take long to figure out why they came.

They were already on the couch in the reception area, kissing and fondling and unbuttoning buttons and making those little noises that don't exist anywhere in the universe except at times like this.

The man wasn't the lawyer, Trench.

His voice was different.

It was deeper, less whiney.

Wilde's best guess was that the woman—*Gina, baby*—worked in the office. Either she or the man or both of them were married. This was their safe haven, their temporary paradise, their walled refuge away from prying eyes.

Wilde settled in.

At the rate they were going, the whole thing would be over in fifteen minutes. With any luck they wouldn't hang around for a smoke or, worse, round two.

Wilde had to admit, the woman sounded good.

She had an animalistic nature.

She wasn't shy.

She knew what she wanted and the man was giving it to her, hard.

What did she look like?'

Wilde fought the urge to crawl out and sneak a peek. He forced himself to stay where he was. Every sound, every moan and every twist sent a new image into his brain. He could picture their exact positions and what each was doing to the other.

Then something unexpected happened.

He noticed a small wooden compartment in that narrow space between the side of the desk and the back end of a drawer, all in all about the size of a briefcase. On closer examination it had a hinged wooden door, hardly differentiable from the wood of the desk. To get anything in or out of the compartment, you'd have to crawl under the desk.

It had no lock.

He opened it.

Inside were a number of file folders.

He pulled one out.

It related to Rojo.

38

With the files on the seat next to him, the hatchet under the files and a storm in his veins, Wilde tipped south back across the river into Paso del Norte where he parked a block away from Rio's place and closed the gap on foot.

He rapped on the door.

No one answered.

He tried the doorknob to see if it was locked. It wasn't. He pushed the door open, heard the shower running and poked his head into the bathroom just far enough to make sure the woman wasn't lying dead in a pool of blood.

She wasn't; anything but.

She had her back to him with her arms up lathering her hair. The curves of her exotic mocha body came in and out of focus through a transparent shower curtain as she water splashed against it. A soft song came from her lips, something Mexican, something he'd never heard before, something hypnotic and sexy.

He lit a cigarette, slumped into a chair, and flipped through the files, all of which on closer examination related to projects Trench was doing or had done for Rojo.

It was the Rojo cache.

One was labeled Bryson Wilde.

Inside were Trench's notes—getting contacted by Rojo to hire someone to kill Wilde, hiring the boxer first, who ended up dead, then hiring two other men afterwards, who also ended up dead; getting contacted by Rojo to come up with a plan to lure Wilde down into Mexico; contacting the Denver lawyer, Jack Strike, with instructions for him in turn to hire Wilde to deliver a briefcase to Trench; the whole sick scenario, it was all there, every stinking two-bit piece of it. There was nothing new, nothing Wilde didn't already know.

The only thing new about it was the fact it was in writing. As evidence in a court of law, it was enough to sink Trench into a legal grave so deep and absolute that he'd never get out.

Trench wasn't the problem, though; not the immediate one in any event.

Rojo was.

Wilde flipped deeper into the stack, hoping beyond hope to find what he was after.

Then, bingo!

He came to a file labeled Maria.

The notes inside indicated that Trench himself had been the one to physically transport the little soul to the custody of a Tijuana man named Poncho Pinch. A ledger indicated that Trench sent money to the man every month. The most striking part of the file was a photograph, a striking black-and-white photograph of Sudden Dance holding the little girl when she was just a tiny little thing.

The joy on Sudden Dance's face belonged to a mother.

It was absolute.

It was nature itself.

Okay, so now he knew where to find the child. The window of opportunity, though, was short. Tomorrow was Monday and in the morning Trench would head to his office. He'd see the window Wilde had to break to get in. He'd look under his desk to make sure the Rojo files were still intact.

They wouldn't be there.

Then he'd figure out what happened.

He'd call Rojo.

Either Rojo or Trench would make a frantic call to the man down in Tijuana, Poncho Pinch, who in turn would whisk the child to someplace new where she couldn't be grabbed.

Thinking it through, there was only one good option.

The Rojo files needed to be intact under the desk when Trench checked for them.

The shower turned off.

"You have company," Wilde shouted.

"Is that you?"

"Yes."

"Give me a minute."

Two minutes later she emerged from the bathroom with a white towel draped around her body, running a comb through long wet hair. She came to Wilde and straddled his lap. "I have something good for you," she said. "I know where Rojo lives."

"You do?"

She nibbled on his ear.

"Yes."

"Tell me."

"I don't want to," she said.

"Why not?"

"Because then you'll go there and then you'll die."

Wilde went to deny the last part of it.

No words came out.

"You were singing a song in the shower," he said.

"Yes."

"It was nice."

"Do you want me to sing it to you?"

The answer surprised him.

"Yes."

39

August 11
Sunday Afternoon

Wilde let a few rays of hope into his heart. The possibility of recovering Maria was tangible. Wilde was still alive and, to the best of his knowledge, so was Jori-Rey. The big trick now was to get Jori-Rey loose from the clutches of Rojo, get to Tijuana to recover the child, and then get Mexico the hell and gone out of their lives forever.

He lit a smoke, gave Rio a kiss on the cheek and headed for the blue piece-of-crap pickup with the Rojo files under his arm.

Getting them back under Trench's desk shouldn't be a problem.

The window was already broken.

He knew the lay of the land.

He wouldn't need to be inside for more than a minute.

The secretary, or whoever she was—*Gina, baby*—already had her daily fix.

The day was hot.

The sun was high.

The humidity was thick.

No one was following him.

At the truck he slid in and put the files on the seat, careful to keep them in order. The engine cranked over. As aesthetically offensive as the vehicle was, Wilde had to admit it hadn't let him down, at least not yet, which is more than he could say for his little foreign job.

Blondie.

Blondie.

Blondie.

Hopefully she was actually getting repaired instead of rotting to an even deeper death at the side of the road.

The miles clicked off.

In his pocket was a crude map drawn by Rio, showing the location of Rojo's establishment, which was something in the nature of a walled villa at the end of a winding dirt road ten kilometers south of the city.

This afternoon, Wilde needed to figure out a way to scope it out. Then tonight, after dark, he needed to get Jori-Rey out of there.

Up ahead on the road three large black ravens picked at road kill. Wilde slowed as he got closer but even with that they didn't want to give up their prize and hung on, almost with defiance.

Wilde steered around, casting his eye on the meal.

It was a squashed cat.

The fur had been pulled away.

Bloody red internals hung out.

When he looked up something in the rearview mirror caught his attention.

A pickup truck was behind him.

Inside were three men.

They looked rough.

Wilde's chest pounded.

He had the hatchet but no gun.

He took a left at the next turn.

The other vehicle followed.

He pushed the gas to the floor.

The streets flew by.

The city got smaller, the country got bigger.

Then gunfire came from behind.

A rear tire blew and the pickup twisted violently to the left. Wilde jerked the wheel the opposite direction only to throw the vehicle into a violent death flip.

40

August 11
Sunday Evening

Wilde woke from a deep cavernous uncon-sciousness to find himself on a mattress, alone in a windowless room. Judging by the cramp in his neck he'd been there for some time.

Where was he?

His thoughts were foggy and he had to force the images to the surface. With increasing clarity he re-membered the death-roll in the pickup, the gas tank bursting into flames, the three men pulling him out and forcing him into their truck, then injecting him in the neck with a needle.

Now he was in a strange room.

He muscled to his feet.

The movement sent sting and snap into his brain.

Whatever he'd been injected with still had a grip on him.

In a corner was a table. In the other was a toilet and a shower.

A large wooden door was closed and wouldn't open.

He pounded on it.

"Let me out!"

No one answered.

The room spun.

His legs wobbled.

He got back down on the mattress before he fell. Then he closed his eyes and let the blackness come. It felt good. It felt right. Everything was beginning to disappear and he didn't fight it.

The next time he woke could have been ten minutes or ten hours later. Either way things were better, much much better. The pain in his head was gone, the room was stable and instead of exhaustion he felt almost refreshed.

He took a long piss, warmed the shower to temperature and stepped in. The spray was an oasis. It brought clarity and restored his soul to where it needed to be.

Clean clothes were on the sink; a pair of tan cotton pants, a white button down shirt and black socks.

He dried off and tried them on.

They fit.

He knew where he was, namely somewhere in crazy Rojo's compound. There was no other explanation. Those were Rojo's men who captured him; no one else had the motive or the audacity. He had one thought and one thought only, namely to let whatever was going to happen start now.

He pounded on the door, not frantically like before, more in the nature of an announcement that he was conscious.

"Hey, let me out of here."

Nothing happened, not for a few heartbeats, and then the faint sound of voices became audible.

A minute later the door opened.

What he saw he couldn't believe.

41

August 11
Sunday Evening

The door led to a larger room, also window-less but very eloquently ordained with expensive furniture, rich textures, intricately woven rugs and a crafted wooden ceiling. That's not what drew Wilde's attention though.

A table along one wall contained an assortment of foods, wines and spirits. That also wasn't what drew his attention.

What drew his attention were the two curvy beauties.

Men would sail the world and fight monsters of every size just to lick their feet, that's the kind of women they were.

They were there for him.

They were his last meal.

"Do you speak English?"

No, they didn't.

One walked over to a clock on the wall, which read slightly after seven. She put an index finger on the minute hand and ran it in a circle to eight, and then another half circle to eight-thirty.

Then she opened her dress and approached him.

The other did the same.

Food, wine and beauty; Wilde could have as much of it as he could consume for the next hour and a half.

He waved the women off.

He needed to think.

He needed to be honest to Jori-Rey.

"Go," he said.

They looked at each other, uncertain.

"Go."

There must have been something final in Wilde's eyes because the woman went to the door at the far end, knocked and got let out.

The door locked behind them.

Wilde was alone.

He ate, concentrating on the lighter foods and resisting the urge to gorge.

He let the liquor sit.

At 8:30 the door would open.

Whatever he had a chance to do, it would be then.

He needed to be ready for it.

Seconds passed, then more. Wilde's eyes stayed almost entirely on the clock, as if it was a death-possessed demon that would lunge at him if he neglected it for even a second.

Now it was 7:30.

Now it was 7:40.

Now it was 7:45 . . .

42

August 11
Sunday Evening

After all the seconds and minutes passed and it was time for whatever was going to happen to happen, three gorillas with pistols opened the door and waved him out. They'd seen rougher than him plenty times before and knew how to stay positioned to where he couldn't grab one of their guns or make a move.

A crowd was outside, drunk and out of control.

Someone shouted something, faces turned to Wilde, and whooping and shouting lit the air, all in Mexican. Wilde didn't understand a word of it.

He knew the tenor though.

The tenor was extreme.

It was final.

It was the way someone yelled at a dog before beating it to death with a bat.

Wilde's chest pounded.

There were too many people.

There was no way out.

Even if he made a move past someone there were ten more to grab him. He couldn't be more stuck if he was in quicksand up to his throat.

Then he saw something that charged every molecule of his body with terror.

It was a large wooden pole sticking out of the ground, something in the nature of a telephone pole except not as high. Four or five feet off the ground was a small platform. Jori-Rey was standing on the platform, roped with her back against the pole and her arms tied high above her head. Her dress was ripped open and pulled down to her waist. Her chest was bare. A blue bandana gagged her mouth.

Her eyes locked on Wilde.

They were nothing but panic.

Wilde must have flinched because the men grabbed him with iron fists and worked him towards the pole. Attached to it at the bottom was a rope thirty feet long. Wilde knew what was coming and fought against it.

The fight was futile.

The men securely tied the rope around his ankle and then they got out of distance. The crowd circled around, keeping back just far enough to where Wilde couldn't get anyone no matter where he might go.

Then came a chant.

Rojo!

Rojo!

Rojo!

Suddenly Rojo appeared.

Wilde's legs weakened.

The man wore no shirt. His chest belonged to a gorilla. His shoulders were wide. His arms were twice as big as Wilde's and ripped with bulging veins. Rojo walked toward the pole, his arms up in salute to the crowd, turning and twisting to let everyone get a good look at him.

Voices rose as one.

A la muerte!

A la muerte!

The man tied a rope to his ankle, identical to Wilde's.

They were both locked in.

Neither could escape the other.

Two men emerged from the crowd, each carrying a burlap sack. One went to Wilde and the other went to Rojo. In unison they dumped the contents to the dirt.

A hatchet fell next to Wilde's foot, a hatchet tethered to a rattlesnake, just like at the hotel. The same thing fell at Rojo's foot.

A la muerte!

A la muerte!

43

August 11
Sunday Evening

Wilde had one thought and one thought only, namely to get the hatchet in hand. He pulled off his shirt and threw it over the snake's head. It landed off-center, covering for only a heartbeat before the snake was out, now coiled in a kill posture a few inches from the hatchet.

The tail rattled.

The head bobbed.

The tongue flicked.

Wilde had been warned.

He'd been warned to death.

He cast an eye to Rojo. The snake was similarly coiled but farther from the hatchet. With a lightning move, Rojo grabbed the hatchet and swung it up. The snake jerked off the ground. Rojo swung it around in a circle over his head two, three, four times and then snapped the line back. The snake ripped in half. The parts flew off and landed in the crowd.

Rojo looked at Wilde.

He slowed down.

He carefully removed the tether from the hatchet, taking his time.

He was in no danger.

He twirled the hatchet into the air and caught it by the handle when it came down.

Wilde kicked at the hatchet, intent on getting it far enough away from the snake to grab it. The reptile struck. It's fangs sunk into Wilde's boot. To his amazement it didn't draw back, not for a second, not for two, not for five. Instead it twisted its body frantically, stuck.

Wilde kicked.

The snake didn't dislodge.

He kicked again, snapping back this time.

The snake's mouth ripped off and the body catapulted in the direction of Rojo, who chopped in half mid-air as it flew past.

Wilde wedged the head off using his other foot.

Then he grabbed the hatchet and faced Rojo.

His heart pounded with the force of a million maniac drums.

Rojo squared off for a second.

Then he let out a blood-curdling war cry and charged.

They swung at each other, each barely missing, again and again and again and again and again. Then Rojo landed a blow, not to Wilde's flesh but to his weapon. Steel exploded on steel and a shock shot up Wilde's arm, a shock so intense and severe that his fingers opened and the weapon flew out of his hand. Before he could recover it, Rojo had already kicked it into the crowd.

Wilde backed up, feet squared, faced to Rojo.

The crowd tensed.

The kill was at hand.

Rojo didn't take it, not yet.

Instead he backed up to the pole and ripped Jori-Rey's dress until it came down. He cut her thigh with the hatchet, not deep, just enough to draw a line of blood.

Fire exploded in Wilde's blood.

He charged.

Rojo was already waiting for him.

He swung.

The hatchet stuck Wilde in the ribs but wasn't blade first.

Pain exploded; untamed and untamable.

The damage was bad.

Ribs were broken.

He couldn't lift his arm.

He couldn't get air into his lungs.

Before he even knew how it happened, he was on the ground. Rojo twisted him onto his back, straddled his chest and pinned him down with his weight.

The man smiled.

He drew the hatchet back and forth in front of Wilde's face like the dance of a snake's head, each motion another declaration that Wilde was totally and absolutely powerless.

He squirmed.

It did no good.

The crowd shouted in unison.

A la muerte!

A la muerte!

Rojo waved the hatchet in the air.

The crowd screamed.

It was here!

The kill was here!

Rojo looked into Wilde's eyes. What Wilde saw was the devil himself. The man twisted his face with hate and then raised the hatchet up into a chopping position with both hands on the handle.

Wilde's body convulsed.

It did no good.

He couldn't twist out, not an inch.

Rojo said, *A la muerte!*

Then he swung the blade down.

44

August 11
Sunday Evening

Suddenly a gun erupted.

Rojo's face exploded.

His body fell back.

Wilde wiggled out from under the weight.

When he looked behind to see who fired the shot, he couldn't believe who he saw. It was the singer from the band Saturday night, the rough guy with the long black hair and the red bandana.

He fired into the air twice to warn the crowd, which was already moving like an anthill that a big boot had come down on. Someone raised a gun, fired at him and got him in the leg. He fired back, got the man in the chest and swung the gun at the crowd.

Everyone ran.

Wilde grabbed the hatchet out of Rojo's filthy dead fingers, got the rope off his ankle and cut Jori-

Rey down.

Then they ran.

They made it to a vehicle, a ratty white pickup. The singer shoved the keys into Wilde's hands, got his body and bloody leg into the back seat and said, "Rapidamente!" The clutch wouldn't go into first. Wilde forced it into second and worked it up to speed without stalling out. Then he got the hell out of there. Another car gave chase but a bullet from the singer's gun shattered the windshield and ran it into a ditch. It happened too fast to tell if the driver got hit or not.

They didn't care.

They made it across the border and holed up in fleabag motel on the outskirts of town, hiding the truck in the back.

The singer spoke no English.

Jori-Rey talked to him in Spanish as she bandaged his leg.

Wilde didn't understand a word of it.

Then something happened that he didn't expect.

Jori-Rey cried, not a sad cry, a happy heartfelt one.

She hugged Wilde with every molecule in her body and said, "Sudden Dance is alive!"

"That can't be."

"No, she is! She really is!"

The story that came from the singer's mouth was a strange and twisted one. He was Sudden Dance's lover, the man who took her to heaven in a way that Rojo never would and could.

They were in love.

She was two months pregnant with his child.

When she started to show—which would be soon—Rojo would kill her and, worse, her first baby, Maria, wherever she was.

Time was ticking.

They devised a plan.

Sudden Dance was scheduled to pick up money in Denver. Her plan was to fake her death while she was there with the hope of getting out of Rojo's life without him killing Maria in retaliation.

By fate she met a woman while having coffee in a place called the Down Towner. The woman she met was a waitress there by the name of Nicole Fountain. They hit it off. Sudden Dance asked the woman if she'd like to make some money. The answer was what she hoped for. That night they met and came up with a plan, most of which was devised by Nicole.

Nicole knew about a drummer who would be playing at a place called the Bokoray on Saturday night. The guy—whose name was Bryson Wilde—had a distinctive car, a small foreign job. He always parked in the alley. At the end of the night he always helped the band pack up before he went home.

Sudden Dance would go to the club that night.

She'd come on to the man. She'd be seen with him all night. She'd let him buy her drinks and get her drunk. He'd make her think she'd go back to his place with him after the show. At the end of the evening she'd find a way to wait for him in his car while he packed up the band.

Nicole would be in the club with friends.

She'd separate from the group at the end of the evening.

She'd join Sudden Dance at the man's car.

They'd drive out into the county where her car would already be waiting.

They'd plant blood and clothing and make it look like a crime had been committed.

The next day Nicole would hire an investigator by the name of Nicholas Dent, ostensibly worried because she had witnessed a murder after leaving the Bokoray. She'd let Dent made a report to the police, leaving her name out of it. That way the police would get the report but she wouldn't be in a position of directly lying to them.

She'd be committing no crime.

The police would investigate it as an actual murder.

The word would eventually get back to Rojo.

He'd believe that his wife was legitimately dead.

It was important that Sudden Dance and the singer not leave Paso del Norte at the same time. It might spark suspicion in Rojo. He might suspect the connection and kill Maria for spite.

The plan was for the singer to leave in three or four months. In the meantime Sudden Dance would hire an investigator to see if she could find out where Maria was.

Sudden Dance told no one about the plan, not even her sister, Jori-Rey. She later learned that Jori-Rey had made her way down to Paso del Norte and was in Rojo's clutches. The singer promised to rescue her, if he could.

The man checked the bandage on his leg and stood up to test it. Then he looked at Wilde and said something in Mexican.

Wilde questioned Jori-Rey.

"What'd he say?"

"He said you don't owe him anything," she said. "He wasn't there to save you, he was there to save me. He was hoping you'd be able to kill Rojo without him having to get involved."

Wilde exhaled.

"Tell him I know where Maria is," he said. "She's being held in Tijuana by a man named Poncho Pinch."

She translated for the singer.

He looked into Wilde's eyes and bowed his head in appreciation. Then he said something to Jori-Rey, gave her a kiss on the cheek and hobbled towards the door.

"Where's he going?" Wilde said.

"Tijuana."

Wilde lit a cigarette, two in fact, and handed one to Jori-Rey. Then he said, "Should we go with him?"

"Yes."

Wilde blew smoke.

"I was afraid you'd say that."

DAY

TEN

August 12
Monday

45

August 12
Monday Evening

The road to Tijuana was bumpy and rough and filled with bathroom stops and humidity and dust and a temperamental radiator that liked to bend the temperature gauge to the H. In spite of it all they made it to here, ten miles outside of town, at a one pump, broken-back gas station that said Petro in red paint on a weathered wooden sign.

The evening shadows were getting long but the air still radiated.

Jori-Rey's skin glistened with sweat.

While a greasy man in a dirty shirt filled the tank, Wilde spotted a scorpion in the brush and wandered over to take a look.

The tail was up.

The stinger was poised.

He'd been warned.

Jori-Rey joined him, wiped her brow with the back of her hand and said, "Do you hate Sudden Dance?"

The answer came easy.

"She set me up," he said. "She used me. Because of her I almost got killed ten times over." He nudged the scorpion with his foot and added, "This little guy here is a lot nicer."

"That's what I thought you'd say."

"There's nothing else to say. She is what she is. I know she's your sister and all and you two are close, but that's the way I feel. I don't ever want to see her. I'm afraid of what I'd say."

"She's not all bad. There's something she did that you're not aware of," she said.

"Something good?"

"Yes."

"Like what?"

"She came back to Denver to save you."

Wilde wrinkled his brow.

"No, she never came back."

"Yes she did," Jori-Rey said. "She heard about that detective Johnnie Fingers going after you. She came back to show him she wasn't actually dead, if it came to that. She wasn't going to let you go down even if it meant giving up the fact that she was still alive."

Wilde shrugged.

"If that's true then she never made any contact with him."

"No, but she made contact with you. She was by your side and ready to act if she had to."

She shook his head.

"No she was never by my side. She never came back. If she told you that she was lying."

"She was by your side," Jori-Rey said. "She still is."

Wilde looked at her with all the confusion he could muster and said, "I have no idea what you're talking about."

"There is no Jori-Rey," she said. "There is only me, Sudden Dance."

"You're Sudden Dance?"

"Yes."

"You expect me to believe that?"

"It's true."

"Then who's the singer?"

"He's someone I paid money to on the side," she said.

"He's not a lover?"

"No. His job was to save me if I ever needed to be saved."

"You mean from Rojo?"

"Yes."

Wilde pulled up an image of Rojo's face splattering into oblivion from a bullet.

"Well, he did his job."

The woman took his hand and held it.

"Wilde, everything else I told you was true," she said. "I needed you to know this last final thing. I didn't want to have any more secrets from you. Do you hate me?"

Wilde tapped two cigarettes out of a pack, set a book of matches on fire and lit them up. He handed one to the woman, who didn't put it to her lips.

She was motionless, waiting for his answer.

The cigarette dangled in her fingers.

Smoke twisted up.

Wilde took a deep drag, blew out and said, "Do I hate you? The truth is, I don't know and I don't want to know. What I do know, though, is that I'm in crazy love with Jori-Rey and I don't ever want to lose her for any reason. So I'm just going to keep calling you that if it's all the same to you."

She put her arms around him and laid her head on his chest.

"Sure."

"Good."

He studied the horizon.

"Let's go get your little girl," he said. "It's time."

ABOUT THE AUTHOR

R.J. Jagger (that's a penname, by the way) is the author of over twenty hard-edged mystery and suspense thrillers. In addition to his own books, Jagger also ghostwrites for a well-known, bestselling author. He is a member of the International Thriller Writers as well as Mystery Writers of America.

RJJAGGER.com

CPSIA information can be obtained
at www.ICGtesting.com
Printed in the USA
BVHW031353210520
580082BV00001B/67